WAITING FOR THE BEATLES

by

Frank Kenny

Chapter One
WAITING

Docker communities were built around the place of work,
jobs were kept in the family and the interaction of social
and working life did produce loyalties and protective
practices, which were based on casualism and justified by
its perpetuation.

D, F, Wilson, *Dockers, The Impact of Industrial Change*

John's mouth only ever dropped open when he was
watching cartoons or waiting to receive Holy Communion. But
now, as he watched the gangs of teenagers square up to each other,
one gang predominantly black, the other all white, his mouth was
wide open. The gangs faced each other across twenty yards of
neutral ground. Eleven-year-old John Cleary and a line of boys sat
on a wall and watched. A gang member pulled out a knife.

Mike Costello, John's friend, pointed and elbowed John in
the ribs.

'Let's stand up?' he said.

John shook his head and held onto the top of the wall.

The battleground was a building site, edged with wire
netting. A large billboard proclaimed the builders, "Tompkins",
and below, "Saint Martin's RC Secondary Modern School.
Completion date September 1964". Underneath that had been
scrawled, "Whites only".

A member of the black gang stepped forward, holding an
Alsatian dog on a rope lead. The dog barked and snarled while
those around it cheered. John was having second thoughts about

watching the fight. When he and Mike had come to watch the gangs before there had been fewer boys, and he had sat further away on the wall and was able to run off when the battle broke into individual fistfights and spiralled around the building site. He had also known most of the other spectators, but now he found he didn't know most of those who watched. Supporters of the black gang - boys of similar age to John's group – shouted abuse at the white gang and even directed their insults towards the white boys who supported them.

Gang members banged sticks on the ground. The dog barked louder. A bottle smashed near the dog; cheers went up from the white gang. A stick was thrown at a white gang member who swung a chain. More bottles were thrown as the gangs screamed, swore and moved closer to each other. John caught sight of a bottle as it looped up high towards him. He turned, grabbed Mike and jumped. Before he reached the ground the bottle smashed on the top of the wall; shards of glass hit the side of John's face and caught in his hair. The two boys ran; other boys on the wall followed their lead. As they ran, more bottles smashed behind them. The dog barked louder.

When the two boys stopped they were out of breath.

'That was friggin' great,' said Mike. 'Bleedin' great that, wasn't it? Did ya see that bottle? Did ya see it? Bleedin' great!'

'I nearly got my head smashed off!' said John, taking a deep breath.

'I know, great wasn't it?' said Mike, 'Friggin' great. Shall we go again?'

John felt the glass in his hair. 'Do you know where we are?' he asked.

'Er, I think so,' said Mike.

John didn't know why he asked. He knew Mike would say that.

'Where are we then?' he said.

Mike turned his head slowly. He gave the impression of trying to deal with an insurmountable problem as he looked up and down the street. John didn't know whether to laugh or punch him.

'Er, I don't know.'

John couldn't understand why he asked Mike questions when he knew that Mike wouldn't know the answer.

They passed a group of black people and John knew then that they must still be near the school. He recognised a pub, "The Volunteer".

'I know where we are; we're by my Uncle Jim's. Come on.'

Black and white neighbours sat chatting in front of red-brick terraced houses, their faces turned to the last of the late evening sun. Mike stared. As the boys drew closer to Uncle Jim's, they heard a guitar and singing through an open window. Mike frowned at the sound.

'What's all that?' he asked.

'Uncle Jim.'

'*Uncle Jim?*'

The front door was open. Uncle Jim sat in the parlour with his back to the window. John knocked on the door and called, 'Uncle Jim! Auntie Sheila!'

Auntie Sheila appeared from the back room, wiping her hands on her pinny. She smiled.

'Hello John. Your uncle's in the parlour, as if you couldn't hear him.' She looked at Mike, and smiled again. She opened the door to the parlour and the sound of the guitar playing poured out. She winced at the sound and shouted, 'Jim! Jim! Your Kathleen's lad's here.'

The boys went in. Uncle Jim balanced the guitar on his knee. He smiled, winked at the boys and put his plectrum on the arm of the chair.

'Well, well, well, young John Cleary. Come in, come in! What a sight for sore eyes. I haven't seen you since -' he scratched the side of his face and rubbed the stubble on his chin - 'I haven't seen you since… the day before yesterday.' He laughed and John laughed with him.

Auntie Sheila spoke from the doorway, 'Would you like something to drink?'

'Yeah,' said Mike.

Uncle Jim pointed at Mike with the neck of the guitar. 'I've seen him before.'

'Yeah,' said John. 'Mike. Mike Costello. He's my mate. He lives in our street.'

'Arthur Costello's lad?' asked Uncle Jim.

'Yeah. Do you know my dad?'

'He's not in my gang but I've worked with him.' Uncle Jim stood his guitar at the back of the armchair. 'So what brings you up to this neck of the woods?'

John guessed his uncle knew the reason. He looked away towards the chimney breast and the shelves that had been fitted between the recesses, each shelf packed with records and books. John turned back while Uncle Jim waited for an answer.

Mike spoke, 'We've been up at the school, near Windsor Street, to see them fighting.'

'Them?' asked Uncle Jim.

'Yeah. *Them*, them fighting *us*.'

'*Them*? *Us*?'

Mike rubbed his thighs with the palms of his hands. He was getting ready to tell Uncle Jim. But Uncle Jim already knew.

'Yeah,' said Mike excitedly. 'Them, them Sambos. Fighting them. Ya know the gangs. The Shines fighting the Jays.'

'Oh.' Uncle Jim scratched his cheek with one finger, 'That *Them*. That *Us*.'

He turned to John. 'Does your mam know you're up here?'

'I'm not sure.'

'I wouldn't like to be in your shoes if she finds out. Does your mam know where you are, Mike?'

'Nar.'

Auntie Sheila came in with two glasses of orange juice and a plate of biscuits on a tray.

'Look at me forgetting my manners,' said Uncle Jim, 'sit down, sit down.'

Mike grabbed a glass and a couple of biscuits. John watched his uncle watch Mike as Mike ate the biscuits and grabbed two more. Uncle Jim smiled. 'Hungry?'

Mike looked up; he had just put another biscuit in his mouth. He nodded, and took a large gulp of orange juice. Uncle Jim's smile grew wider. He rubbed his chin. John leaned past Mike and picked up his glass.

'It's getting late and looking at you two has given me a thirst,' said Uncle Jim, 'Finish that off and I'll walk you down as far as the pub. I'll go and get my coat.'

Mike finished his orange juice, picked up another biscuit and went over to the shelves. He pulled a record out and looked at the sleeve. 'Muddy Waters?' He pushed the record back and pulled out another. 'Lightning Slim Hopkins? These names are daft.' He put the record back, picked up Uncle Jim's guitar and pretended to play.

'Put it down', said John.

Mike put the guitar down and looked at the books; he pulled one out and put it back. A small bronze bust of Lenin sat on a shelf. Mike held it up. 'Who's this?' he asked.

'I don't know.'

'You don't *know*?'

'No, I don't soddin' *know*. Put it back.' Mike replaced the bust. John picked up a boxing magazine and flicked through it. He wished he hadn't brought Mike to his uncle's. He knew he would act like this.

He heard Auntie Sheila's voice in the next room. She shouted. Uncle Jim replied. Auntie Sheila shouted again. John heard the words 'pub' and 'money'.

Mike said, 'What's all that about?'

'They always argue. Sometimes Uncle Jim goes to the pub and Auntie Sheila doesn't like it. Sometimes, after the pub he comes to our house and sleeps on the couch.' John gave a shrug. They both sat down.

Uncle Jim came in as if nothing had happened. He clapped his hands. 'Ready lads?'

Mike picked up the last biscuit off the plate as they left.

As they stepped into the street Uncle Jim spoke to John.

'Is your mam still making you go to Church?'

'She doesn't make me, I go 'cause I want to.'

'Yeah, that's right, I forgot.' He turned to Mike. 'Do you go to Saint Pat's school like John?'

'No, Saint Malachy's,' John answered for Mike, 'our street's on the border of Saint Pat's and Saint Malachy's parishes, so some kids in our street go to one school and some go the other.'

'What about next week?' said Uncle Jim, 'Are you going to see The Beatles when they come into town?' He played an imaginary guitar.

'Yeah,' said John.

'Dead right,' said Mike.

'There'll be thousands up there. Is your mam letting you go, John?'

'Yeah.'

'Have you asked your mam, Mike?'

'I don't have to ask.'

A black couple sat outside the house opposite. Uncle Jim waved. The man raised a hand. Uncle Jim noticed Mike stare at the couple. They came to the corner of the street.

'See that street sign?' said Uncle Jim. 'Pilgrim Street. That street was named after a privateer. That's like a pirate ship that sailed on the side of the King, over a hundred years ago. Lots of streets in Liverpool are named after ship owners, merchants and Admirals. There was this one place, the Goree, a big rock where the ships used to meet the slave traders, off the coast of a place called Cape Verde. They'd buy the slaves, or exchange them for stuff on the ship; things that had been made in England. Then they'd go the West Indies and trade the slaves for sugar and rum. Have you heard about the ship 'Zong'? Funny name but not funny what happened.'

'Why, what happened?' asked Mike.

'Do you really want to know?' Uncle Jim slowed down.

'Yeah.'

'The 'Zong' was a slaver. It sailed from Cape Verde. Exchanged muskets, bundles of cloth, even beer. All for African slaves. Anyway, the captain of the 'Zong' wasn't much cop and after the exchange when he set sail for the West Indies, he managed to get the ship lost. They were lost for a good while and started to run low on rations. Time passed and they still couldn't find their bearings, then they began to starve. So what do you think they did?'

'Started fishing?' suggested John. 'Tried to kill a whale?'

'No. You're thinking, though. It would have been better if they could have done that. What it was, see, they had a company rule. A slave died, they lost the money for him. Do you understand?'

'Yeah, I understand. Couldn't they go back or ask another ship for food?'

'No. No other ships about and they'd gone too far. They'd be off the main trade routes. Like I said before, the captain had got them lost; he probably couldn't find his arse in a dark room with both hands. Excuse my language, lads. They had a company regulation: if you lost a slave, you lost your money, remember?'

'Yeah,' said Mike.

'So what did they do?' said Uncle Jim. He stopped walking.

'Turn back,' said Mike.

'No, too far out at sea; the captain had lost the trade winds. The rule was if a slave died you lost your money. But if you had to throw slaves overboard, to lighten the load, for the safety of the ship, you got paid for the slave. So what did the captain do?'

John looked at Mike. Mike looked at Uncle Jim.

'He threw the slaves overboard,' said Uncle Jim.

'The dead ones?' said Mike

'No the live ones.'

'They threw them off the boat into the sea,' asked John, 'when they were alive?'

'No, not a boat John, a ship. A boat's what you row on Sefton Park Lake. But yes, they threw them off when they were alive.'

'Why?' asked Mike.

'Money, I just told you.'

'How many slaves were thrown in the sea?' asked Mike.

'Over one hundred!'

'Couldn't they swim after the ship, hold on to it?' asked John.

'No. Apparently the captain was a lousy navigator, but a good Christian. He kept the chains on the slaves so they'd drown quicker.' Uncle Jim stopped and bent down into Mike's face.

'Are you a good Christian, Mike?'

Mike opened his mouth to speak, but nothing came out. Uncle Jim straightened up. Outside the pub a newspaper boy stood next to a sandwich board.

'I'll just get an evening paper,' said Uncle Jim, 'to read with my pint and see what this crowd in the council are up to.'

John glanced at the headlines on the board: "City Council Promises to Build 20,000 New Houses in Next Four Years."

Uncle Jim noticed John looking and laughed to himself.

'City Council! Gangsters, all of them,' he said, then reached into his pocket, pulled out some money and handed it to the boys. 'Here's a few bob, get yourselves some sweets on the way home. And go straight home.'

He waved and went towards the pub. The boys made their way home.

'Does your Uncle always talk like that?' asked Mike.

'Sometimes. He went away to sea for years before going to work on the docks with my dad and our Peter. Uncle Jim's been around the world loads of times.'

'Yeah?'

'Yeah. He stopped going, though.'

'Why?'

'My mam said he was in the union and always causing trouble. Once he was playing his guitar on deck for some of the other men. They'd just finished their shift. An officer on the ship told Uncle Jim to put the guitar away.'

'What happened?'

'Uncle Jim said he wasn't doing any harm, and him and the officer had an argument.'

'Then what happened?'

'Uncle Jim punched the officer, so they locked him up on the ship.'

'In jail?'

'In the brig, that's like a jail on a ship. My mam said Uncle Jim would cause murder in a graveyard. Come on, I'll race you to the end of the road.'

*　　　　　　　*　　　　　　　*

The boys were almost home. They passed a pair of corrugated iron doors: "S. Norton Scrap Metal – Best Prices Paid" had been hand painted across them.

'Hey, remember when we found that lead piping last month in that empty house?' said Mike.

'We didn't find it, did we? Your Steve and his mate made us dig it out the walls; I got bits of plaster all over me.'

'Yeah well, the same thing. Old Mr. Norton gave us a few bob for it, didn't he?'

'It wasn't us he gave it to. It was your Steve that was given the money. All we got was sixpence between us. Him and his mate kept the rest.'

9

'Yeah, but three pence each wasn't bad.'

Mike's shameless defense of Steve's unequal sharing of the money from Mr. Norton made John mad. He had an idea.

'Has anybody been in Jackie Ryan's house looking for scrap yet?'

'No, and there won't be anyone either.' There was an edge to Mike's reply.

John knew any mention of anyone trying to get into Mike's ex neighbours, the Ryans', looking for scrap would upset him. Jackie Ryan was the same age as John, and Jackie's family had accepted an offer from the Corporation for a new house on the outskirts of the city in Halewood. The Ryans had moved a fortnight ago and as far as John knew the corrugated sheets on the windows and doors had kept most of the kids out.

The boys turned into their street. The previous year the Corporation had built new houses, named Laxey Way. There were six blocks with six flats. Each block had a back yard, separated from John's street with wire fencing. The verandas of the flats overlooked their street.

'John! John, over here!'

It was thirteen-year-old Geoffrey Budd. He stood in the backyard of his block, holding a cricket bat. Next to him were twelve-year-old Philip and Elizabeth, who lived in adjoining blocks. John put his head down and picked up his step.

'Bleedin' 'ell, the snobs. What do they want?' asked Mike.

John walked faster.

'John! John, we want to talk to you,' shouted Geoffrey, his face close to the wire netting.

John walked even faster and had to force himself not to break into a run. Mike caught up with him.

'Friggin' 'ell, you're not playing with the snobs are ya?' questioned Mike.

John didn't stop. He kept his head down.

'No, no it's not that... there was no one in the street to play with on Sunday. You'd all gone the park. I was fed up so I swapped some comics with Geoffrey Budd.'

They stopped. Geoffrey was out of sight.

'What?' said Mike.

'I was fed up. I just climbed the fence and swapped a few of my old comics. I was only there five minutes.'

'Well, we don't play with them college puddin's. You know that. And our Steve's waiting to see Geoffrey Budd; he's going to have a fight with him.'

'What for?'

Mike looked at him as if he had two heads. 'What for? Nothing, he's just going to batter him.'

John knew it had been a bad idea swapping comics but it was true; he was bored. Being seen with the snobs, as the rest of the gang in the street called them, was dangerous. And he had been seen, but up to now nothing had been said. If it got out, he could be thrown out of the gang or worse.

John's front door was open. John told Mike he'd call for him after tea and went in. As he stepped into the parlour he could hear the television on in the back room. The family hardly ever used this room. A mirror-backed cabinet stacked with ornaments stood against the wall near the doorway. A large three-piece suite was also in the room. The settee was pushed up against the wall, which faced the cabinet. In front of the settee stood a large polished table and four chairs. The two armchairs each squeezed into a corner. The room measured ten by ten and there was only enough space to move from the front door to the back kitchen. Except for its orderly fashion, the contents of the room could be mistaken for stored furniture ready for removal. There was no door between the parlour and the back room. His dad had removed it. The day after the cabinet was delivered it was found the door knocked against the cabinet. John's mother had ordered its removal.

John sniffed; there was the usual smell of furniture polish. It was strong today, which meant his mother had been polishing since he'd left the house with Mike to see the fights.

In the back room, a tall cupboard stood under the bedroom stairs. His brother Peter sat at a table nearby and read a newspaper. At a large Belfast sink their mother stood washing clothes; the sink was fixed beneath a window. A television stood in the corner near the sink; an armchair sat close to the fireplace. His brother looked up.

'Hiya,' said Peter.

'Hiya,' replied John.

Their mother turned around. 'What time do you call this? Your tea's been in the oven ages. Wash your hands.'
She turned and wrung out some wet clothes.

He went to the sink. 'I called into Uncle Jim's before.'

'Oh, him. That *one*. Was Auntie Sheila there?'

'Yeah, she gave me and Mike Costello something to eat. Then Uncle Jim walked us part of the way home.'

'As far as the pub?'

He dried his hands, 'Er, yeah. I think he was only going in for cigarettes.'

'Don't be telling lies, John. Remember that one for the priest next time you go to confession.'

To John's way of thinking, telling lies was a sin. Lies were not as bad as swear words, but he still had to remember them for the priest at confession. Flippin', soddin', bloomin', friggin' and bleedin' were alright, but he didn't say bleedin', soddin' or friggin' in the house. The other ones were swear words. Even thinking them. That's what the priest had told him.

He sat at the table. Peter lowered his paper, glanced towards their mother then at John and smiled. John looked at him, not amused. He recalled the week Peter began to work with their dad on the docks. Not long after he started in his dad's gang, Uncle Jim had joined them. Uncle Jim had worked on the docks since John could remember, but not with John's dad. Later, a gang member who worked with John's dad had left and Uncle Jim was transferred in. John's mother didn't like the fact that her brother was working so closely with Peter. She'd tell John his Uncle would cause murder wherever he went. John knew he wasn't that bad, but he also knew what his mother meant. Peter told him that when Uncle Jim went away to sea he had often found himself locked up and had missed his ship quite a few times as well. If Uncle Jim liked a port his ship was docked in, then he'd 'take a powder' and never return to ship out. Usually this would happen when he was docked in America. John also knew that his uncle was with the union and that he was a member of the Star Club. All John knew was that it was a club for men who wanted to discuss politics. When his mother found out Peter had been going to the Star Club with Uncle Jim she hit the roof. John had pretended to read a comic while his mother let fly, so his dad got the lot.

'I told you! I told you this would happen!' his mother had shouted. 'You know lots of fellas down on the dock; you've been working down there long enough. You could have got our Jim working with another gang, but no, you never! Now look, the Star Club!'

John's dad never said anything.

*   *   *

After his tea, John went out. His gang stood near a lamp post at the end of the street outside Mike's house. The Dunleavy twins, Kevin and Keith, were the same age as Steve Costello, who was two years older than John and Mike. The twins weren't identical but they both wore glasses. For a while Keith had to wear a plaster that covered one of his lenses, due to a "lazy eye". Mike made a joke and said that Keith had a lazy eye because it wouldn't go to school, but Kevin punched him in the arm.

A rope had been tied to the top of the lamp post as a swing and Steve pushed his seven-year old brother, Tony, who was sitting in it. A gang of small kids waited to have their turn. Tony saw John approach.

'Ah John's a snob,' he cried.

John hesitated for a split second, then forced himself to carry on.

'I'm not.'

'You are, playing with the snobs,' shouted Kevin. 'Ha, snob.'

'I wasn't, honest.'

'Ah, snob, John the snob!'

'I'm not.'

'You were playing with them, our Tony seen ya,' said Steve.

'I wasn't.'

'You calling our Tony a liar?'

Steve grabbed hold of the rope and stopped the swing. It looked like Tony was being called to give a blow-by-blow account of John's treachery. Steve had both his hands on his brother's shoulders. John stared at Steve's hands. Steve was big for his age. Not so much tall as chunky; his features broad, his nose flat, eyes wide apart, shoulders large. From a distance he could easily be mistaken for a young man. But it was his hands placed on Tony's shoulders that mesmerized John. It was as if John had for the first time noticed how big, meaty and calloused they were. He imagined his own puny hand clenched into a fist next to Steve's.

'Er, no, no.' John broke out of his trance. 'I was playing with my tennis ball and it went over their yard. I went to get it back. I asked them had they seen it.'

'Our Tony said, you had comics with you,' said Steve

'Er, yeah, er, yeah. I'd been to Tommy Sanderson's for swaps.'

His gaze went back to Steve's hands. He had to force himself to look away and concentrate on his defence. No one spoke as Steve went up to John and pushed his face into his.

'If you've been playing with them,' Steve half shouted, 'ya not in the gang and we'll fuckin' batter ya.'

John's knees went weak. Any thoughts of adding to his defence drained away. In John's mind the words, 'We'll batter ya' echoed out. Steve was big enough to batter him on his own, but '*We'll* batter ya' - they'd all batter him, even soddin' little Tony. Oh God, Jesus, tonight. And John knew. He knew what he was going to say next. And he tried to stop himself. He pressed his lips together, tried to shut up. He really did try but he couldn't. His mouth opened and he spoke.

'He said he can fight you, Steve.'

'What?'

'Yeah, Geoffrey, I heard him.'

'I'll fuckin' kill him! The bastard!'

John couldn't stop himself. He felt like he was tumbling down a hill.

'And Philip? Philip! He's shaggin' Elizabeth.'

'What?' They all shouted at the same time and looked at each other.

'Tell us,' said Mike.

'What about your Tony and the little ones?'

'Oh yeah.'

John struggled to think of something as a follow-up but nothing happened. Not a thing to say came into his head. He thought of closing his eyes tight to try and concentrate but he knew he couldn't do that. His mind was blank. There was a shout.

'Kevin, Keith! Here ya are! I got this for you today!' It was Mr. Dunleavy. He held a football in one hand and a large empty brown paper bag in the other. 'Catch!' Mr Dunleavy shouted and kicked the ball high into the air. Everyone around the lamp post cheered and ran after it.

Everyone except John, who stood there and said under his breath, 'Thanks God, thanks, thanks, thanks. I'll say extra prayers tonight - I will honest, honest.'

A game of football started.

'Tell us about it, after the footy,' said the older lads.

'Yeah I will,' said John.

John was on Steve's side. John's mother called him in before the game was finished. He didn't even pretend that he wanted to stay out longer, just in case his mother said yes. For the first time he was glad to be called in for bed. The next day he planned to tell the gang that he might not have heard Geoffrey or Philip properly because he was only there for a short while. He might have only heard them swearing. He would get away with it, he told himself.

That night, he couldn't sleep. It was still light outside. He thought back to when Geoffrey, Philip and Elizabeth had moved in, Keith Dunleavy had told John and the others that they were snobs because they talked posh, so no one played with them. They would play cricket in the yard with a tennis ball, just the three of them. They never played football. But when their ball went over the fence, the little kids would run off with it. After a couple of weeks all the little kids in the street had a tennis ball each. Now Geoffrey practiced his batting strokes with an invisible ball.

The story John had told Mike was true. The gang had been out of the street and John's mother had told him off for getting under her feet. So he had gone outside and noticed Geoffrey, Philip and Elizabeth in their back yard. They sat against a small brick shelter used for the bins. They all read comics. John had asked them what the comics were. Geoffrey and Philip read the *Hotspur* and *Beano*, Elizabeth read the *Bunty*.

'If you've got any *DC* or *Marvel* comics I'll swap you,' said John.

'Yes, I have,' said Geoffrey.

'Me too, I have as well,' said Philip.

'Go and get them then, and I'll get mine,' said John.

He'd returned with a dozen comics tucked down the front of his trousers, climbed the fence and they'd swapped. Geoffrey and Philip had three each - old copies which John had read - but he swapped anyway. They had talked and wanted to know about everyone in the street, what kids lived in what house, what school they went to, what their dads' jobs were and where they worked, so he'd told them. He asked them what school they went to. They told him but John had never heard of it, so he guessed it must have been quite a way out of the neighborhood. He couldn't remember, but it didn't sound if it was Catholic because it wasn't saint something or other. John guessed it was a college. He would sometimes see the three of them leave for school, early, dressed in their school uniforms with satchels hung over their shoulders.

Philip asked John, 'Are you Irish?'

Geoffrey and Elizabeth laughed. John felt soft.

'No.'

'Is your mum Irish?'

'No.'

'Is your father?'

'No.' That was all John could think to say. They had giggled, so John had asked, 'Why?'

'It's just that you sound Irish,' said Philip.

John remembered thinking, how can I be friggin' Irish when I live here?

Geoffrey told him, 'We're only living here for a short while until we find a proper house. It's the housing shortage due to the war; supply and demand and all that, you know?'

John thought, 'What's a proper house? Housing shortage; supply and demand; all that, you know.' John certainly didn't know; he never had a clue what Geoffrey was on about and he guessed it must have shown. Whatever it was, Geoffrey said his family would be moving soon. Philip said they were going to move as well but John guessed he was just saying that. They told him where they used to live but he had never heard of the area and had forgotten it almost as soon as they had told him. He told them of the time he went to watch a football match, Liverpool at Anfield, watching it from the Boys' Pen. He guessed he must have gotten excited and been talking too fast, because Geoffrey had shaken his head and said, 'I don't understand a word you're saying.'

Elizabeth had whispered something to Geoffrey and they had both laughed. Philip had laughed too, even though he couldn't have heard her. John stayed a while longer but after that he hadn't said much. Then the three of them had talked between themselves about their school and things John didn't know anything about. John had decided to go when someone shouted.

'Ha, ha, John's playing with the snobs.'

It was Tony Costello. John felt his face burn up.

'I've gotta go now, see yas,' he had muttered.

He hadn't even looked at them as he'd grabbed his comics and flown over the fence. Tony Costello still shouted as he dropped down. He noticed the front door to his house was closed, so he ran to the end of his street and the entry, which would take him to his backyard door and away from Tony's jeers. He felt ashamed; he knew he'd let himself and the gang down.

John rearranged his pillow, put his hands under his head and stared at the ceiling. Light still shone through the window. The light nights reminded him of when he was in hospital. He had been six and he wouldn't stand up straight. His left leg was nearly always bent slightly. His mother kept on telling him to stand up straight and stop bending his leg, but he kept on forgetting. Eventually, she took him to the doctor who told her there was nothing wrong but his mother believed there was. So eventually he saw a specialist at the hospital. He knew his mother was proud of herself for challenging the doctor.

'I wanted a second opinion,' she told him. 'I knew it wasn't right. I kept on praying for you but I still knew there was something wrong. The specialist knew; he knew straight away there was something wrong.'

She'd tell him the story about getting a second opinion and about polio constantly being in the news. So he was admitted to the Children's Hospital. He was given injections in the morning and afternoon. He forced himself to be brave by thinking of the children in the ward who had to wear calipers. He knew his mother must have been worried. After six weeks the doctors declared him fit enough to go home. He wasn't certain what had been the problem. Whatever it was it had been put right, because he didn't stand with his leg bent anymore.

In the hospital, one afternoon before visiting, two nurses had come to his bed with a boy his own age in a wheelchair. They had told him to get out of the bed. He had stood there in his pyjamas and watched as the nurses lifted the boy from his chair and placed him in John's bed. The boy never looked at John. One of the nurses told John to climb into the wheelchair and then pushed him down to the end of the ward into a storeroom without a window. Inside was a large sink with mops and buckets and a smell of bleach; they left him sitting in the wheelchair with the door open. He hadn't seen the nurses before and wished that one particular nurse whom he liked had been on duty; she wouldn't have let him be taken out of his bed.

The parents of the boy visited. The boy's father had a small, pencil-thin moustache and smoked a pipe. His mother wore a fur coat. She took the coat off and slowly glanced around the ward. That afternoon no one from John's family visited. But Marty Jones did. Marty was twenty years old and lived next door but one; he had gone away to sea and was home on leave. Marty entered the ward and was directed to the storeroom. He asked him why he was sitting in a wheelchair in a room full of mops and buckets, so John told him. He felt sorry for himself but Marty just passed him a bag of sweets and started talking. When the bell rang to end visiting, the parents of the boy who was in John's bed were the last to leave. After they had gone, he was wheeled back to his bed and was told to get out of the wheelchair as they prepared to put the boy back in. Again the boy ignored John. The nurses spoke to the boy, and he spoke in the same self-assured manner, just like Geoffrey Budd.

Chapter Two
HALEWOOD

In Liverpool alone some 60 per cent of the city's
205,000 dwellings date from before1920 and in
1961 approximately 79,000 of these were unfit.

D, E, Bain, *Merseyside and the British Economy: the
1930s and the Second World War*

'John,' his mother said as she came down the stairs with an
armful of bed linen for the wash, 'before you go to Halewood with
Mary, go on a message for me.' She dropped the linen near the
sink. 'Go to Cullen's and get me five Woodbines.'

'Can I keep the change?'

'No.'

'I'll just be a minute,' said John as he ran upstairs to the
bedroom he shared with Peter. He opened the bottom drawer of the
wardrobe and pulled out the maracas Marty Jones had brought back
from a sea trip. He pushed the handle up into one of them and rice
poured from the shell. The maracas were painted with blue, yellow
and red hoops and, as the rice poured out, two sixpences and a
small enamel trade union badge slid out with it. The badge had
been Uncle Jim's and he had worn the badge on his lapel when he
went away to sea. John had constantly pestered his uncle for the
badge. And when his uncle eventually gave it to John he made him
promise not to tell John's mother.

John poured the rice, money and badge back into the
maraca and returned it to the drawer. He lifted the linoleum near
the corner of the wardrobe where he had hidden three pennies,

which were too large to fit inside the maraca. John always hid money and anything valuable to him; he didn't think it sly or dishonest, merely a precaution. He believed it was unwise to keep money in his pockets if he didn't have to. It might get lost or his mother or dad might hear the coins jingling and if he were to ask them for money they'd only say, 'You've got money of your own.'

John stared up at the pictures of The Beatles he'd stuck on the wall. Most of them came from Mary's magazines; some of the better ones he'd swapped for comics or toys with boys from school. There were also large individual pictures of each Beatle. John went to the sash window and pushed it up. In the backyard he saw a small piece of dinner plate near the toilet; it was the remains of the plate he'd tried to catch a pigeon with. His mother had given him a telling off that seemed to go on for hours. He knew lots of lads who kept pigeons. He liked the idea of having a pigeon coop in the backyard, of feeding them every day, of grooming them and maybe even racing them. But first he had to catch them.

The previous week he'd collected a piece of string and a stick, and, when his mother wasn't looking, a dinner plate, and had made a bird trap. He'd tied the string to the stick and propped the plate up with it. Then he'd scattered pieces of bread around and under the plate. He'd hidden in the toilet, leaving the door open slightly, and waited without moving. Nothing had happened for what seemed like ages until a pigeon had landed and begun to feed on the bread. John sprung his trap, the pigeon had flown off as soon as the stick moved and the plate had smashed. His mother had shouted at him.

'At least you could have used a pan instead of one of my best plates!'

He went back downstairs, thinking about keeping pigeons and thinking about money.   He tried again.

'After I go to the shop mam, can I keep the change?'

'No.'

'Go on, mam. I'm saving up for when The Beatles come.'

'John, I haven't said you can go yet.'

'Don't joke mam, I'm going.'

'Are you now? And who are you thinking of going with?'

'Mike, their Steve, Kevin and Keith Dunleavy.'

'Well I'd like to talk to Steve or the twins before you go.'

'Why? I can't bring them to the house like a little kid.'

'You can, John.'

'But Mam!'

'Go to the shop! And be careful crossing the road; look both ways, do you hear me?'

'Alright.'

John went out the back way and put the broken piece of plate in the bin. At the rear of John's street were paving slabs and a stone gutter that ran alongside the backyard walls. Mike told him the houses that backed onto their street had been bombed in the war but John's dad had said that they were old and had to be pulled down. Now there was a strip of grass, a "Billy ock", thirty yards wide. It could have been used for football but it was on an incline. The surrounding area rose up from the river and it was only after a mile or so, near to Princes Road that it levelled off.

John passed some smaller kids who were playing on a mound of bricks from a tumbled-down backyard wall. The wall had been part of a house at the top end of his street, which had been empty for a month. The kids had piled the bricks on top of one another and were playing king of the castle. The Corporation had moved the families out of the houses at the other end of his street, which were now empty and awaiting demolition. The kids called the empty houses "bomdies", which puzzled John because the houses hadn't been bombed in the war. They were simply old and empty.

He reached Warwick Street. His own street continued past Warwick Street up to Northumberland Street, where it stopped. His gang didn't hang around with the kids from the other end of the street. There was a pub on the corner called the Warwick Castle but everyone knew it as the "Corner o' Wooley" because it was also on the corner of Woolfe Street. Uncle Jim explained that the street was named after General Woolfe, who had fought the French and the North American Indians. His uncle would also tell him stories about the times he spent away at sea. He told them mainly when he had been in the pub. The only problem was that sometimes he would say something that his sister didn't think John should hear, and she'd tell her brother off. This would develop into an argument. The arguments between them were usually self-contained and hardly ever involved anyone else in the house. Anyone who was about knew by experience that it was best to steer clear of being dragged into the conflicting opinions of brother and sister. Any taking of sides would just be a case of adding fuel to the fire. Not that any of the family would be brave or foolish enough to take Uncle Jim's side. But most of the stories Uncle Jim told John would pass off without incident. He would tell about the early days of the port. He'd told John stories of press gangs that would roam the streets and alleys near the docks. The threat of press gangs became so serious, Uncle Jim had told him, that in the pubs they'd started serving beer in metal mugs that had a glass bottom. The reason for this was that the press gangs were in the habit of slipping a shilling into a man's drink when he wasn't looking. When the man got to the end of his drink he'd see the shilling and take it out. That's the time, said Uncle Jim, when the press gang would strike.

'I see you've taken the King's shilling. Alright, let's be having you.'

'That would be it then; they'd have you. Bang on the head and drag you to the ship. Just think, you say to your missus, "I'm just going for a quick pint, see you later." Next thing is you wake up, a lump on your head the size of a duck egg, and you're half way to Jamaica!'

John learnt of the different kinds of ships that sailed in and out of Liverpool and of the streets in the city that were named after famous people. His uncle had gone away to sea when he left school but all his self-taught knowledge didn't cut any ice with his sister, who told John that her brother would cause murder in an empty room. 'He'd have the last word with Our Lord!'

Her brother would respond by saying that his sister was "too soft"; that even when they were kids she had been too soft with the other kids in the street. John's mother would say, 'There's nothing wrong with being nice to people; being nice never cost anything.'

'Yes Kathleen', Uncle Jim would reply, 'but there's a difference between being nice and being soft. That's our mam's fault, that. Taking you to Church every day, that's what's got you thinking like that.'

'There's nothing wrong with going to Church. You want to go, it would do you good.'

And they would go on like that all the time. John's dad wasn't as religious as John's mother. If John missed Sunday morning mass he went to seven o'clock mass with his dad, who belonged to the Territorial Army. Afterwards his dad would catch a bus to the social club at the barracks. Sometimes, after mass, his dad would buy a block of ice cream for him and Mary. But now Mary wasn't that bothered with ice cream. She was getting a bit too old at fifteen, going to work and smoking. When he was younger she would take him to visit his auntie's. Now though, she called him a "pain" and a "stupid child".

Today it was different; they were going to Halewood to visit one of her friends, Margaret Clarke, who had moved to a new estate on the outskirts of the city. He had a notion that it was his mother who wanted him to go, to keep Mary company.

John checked the money his mother had given him to go to the shop with. A pair of old shops stood next to each other, Cullen's and Elsie's. Elsie's was a fruit and veg' shop that also sold tinned goods. Cullen's was the newsagents his family used; it was only in there that he would be able to buy his mother's cigarettes. He knew Mrs. Cullen would serve him because she knew the cigarettes were for his mother. When he entered, Albie McInerney was in front of him holding a shopping bag, a newspaper and a packet of sweets. Mrs. Cullen helped Albie sort out the money he'd been given to pay for his mother's shopping.

Albie was in his late twenties and lived with his mother. The adults said he was 'retarded.'

John guessed Albie had never had a job, but in the autumn a travelling fair had pitched itself up on the "Hollow", a large level patch of waste ground at the rear of Mill Street. Albie would hang around the fair and the men who ran the fair would tell him to tidy up and keep the kids away from the rides. John guessed that Albie was given some money but to John, that wasn't a proper job. Usually when John saw Albie he was going on an errand for his mother, or hanging around outside the betting shop. Albie would chat with the men who gathered there waiting for the next race and have a cigarette with them. Albie turned around.

'Hiya,' said John.

Albie simply stared at him and walked out of the shop. Sometimes he said hello, sometimes he didn't.

'I'm back, mam!' shouted John as he came through the back door and put the packet of cigarettes on top of the television. 'I've left the change.'

'Thanks lad,' she said and then, looking up from her polishing, she said, 'Oh … keep the change.'

John ran upstairs to his bedroom and put the three pennies under the linoleum with the other three, then he opened the window. He looked towards the docks and the grain silos that sat behind the dockyard wall. When he lay in bed on winter nights, when it became foggy, he could hear the ships' horns blow. He would wrap the bed covers around him tightly and try to think what country the ship might be from. He would try to guess if the ship was sailing in or out of the docks and wonder what its next port would be.

And pigeons constantly flew to and from their nests in and on the silos. One silo was grey concrete. It reminded John of a fat 'T', but upside down. The second was old, built of brick and oblong. It was a dirty sooty black. The silos were over two hundred feet high and three hundred feet long. On summer evenings, the sun would make its way behind the silos and cover the rooftops around the streets with broken shadows. Sometimes John would be looking out of his bedroom window and see his dad coming home from work. He would run down and his dad would give him a swing on his arm. John thought he was getting too big for all that now, but he would still run down to meet him.

Mary shouted up that she was ready to leave and John ran downstairs. Their mother walked them to the door and said, 'You know where you're going to in Halewood, don't you Mary?'

'Yes, I know. I've got a good idea what bus stop to get off at.'

'And don't you two go and get yourselves lost,' John's mother looked at him as she spoke. John had got himself lost before, and he'd no intention of doing it again.

'I won't, mam,' he said.

It took John and Mary two buses to get to Margaret's house. There was a bus into the city centre, followed by a long wait for another one to Halewood. Margaret had lived in Halewood for nearly a month and had written a letter to Mary the week before. When they were on the bus Mary read from Margaret's letter and even let John have a look. When he finished, Mary carefully put the letter back in the envelope and returned it to her coat pocket. She told John that Margaret had been her best friend at school and had felt sad leaving, but Mary had tried to cheer her up.

'Well, now you're going to a brand new house with a front and back garden and you're staying on for the fifth year at a brand new school there'll be trees and fields all around you. Come on, you'll soon make new friends and you can always come back and visit.'

John wasn't sure if Mary wanted to move to the outskirts herself, the way she spoke. He recalled his mother's look at him when she told them not to get lost because once when he was six he had managed to do just that. He had gone to Sefton Park with Mike, Jackie Ryan and Kevin Dunleavy. John had never been there before. They had gone there to play football and afterwards watch the men fish in the lake. After their game of football and when the boys had seen enough of the men casting their lines and occasionally pulling in a fish, they decided to go home. But as they left, Kevin bullied and bossed the younger boys around. He told them he was the one who had taken them to the park and only he knew the way home. He said that if they didn't do as he told them, he would leave them and they'd get themselves lost. It seemed that the more commands Kevin issued and the quicker they complied, the shittier Kevin's attitude became. Eventually, John had turned around and gone off on his own. After half an hour he had found himself in another park he'd never been in before. He'd spent ten minutes there trying to get his bearings and another ten minutes going back around the park, trying to remember which way he had come in. He'd walked faster and faster; and the faster he'd walked, the more he'd thought that he might be lost. When it finally dawned on him that he was lost, he'd asked people in the park, 'Do you know where 68 New Harrington Street, Liverpool 8 is?' 'I'm lost; do you know where 68 New Harrington Street is?' And no one knew, so he was lost and he cried.

Thinking about it now, he felt a bit daft but reasoned he had only been a kid then. He'd eventually asked a couple who didn't know his street, but asked him where it was. They had a Mini, and gave him a ride home. John sat in the back. The husband drove and his wife passed John a handkerchief. He'd dried his eyes and blown his nose and passed the handkerchief back, but the woman told him he could keep it.

About a mile from John's home, the man called at a sweet shop for directions. His wife asked John if he wanted a bar of chocolate. He still had chewing gum in his mouth. He didn't know how he still had his chewing gum with all the crying he had done. When the couple went into the shop he didn't know what to do with the chewing gum. He couldn't chew that and eat the chocolate and he didn't want to swallow it. He had been told that if you swallowed chewing gum it might stick to your heart and you'd die. He didn't believe that now, but he had then. He couldn't throw it out of a window because they were closed. And he didn't want to pass it to one of the couple to throw away, so he had stuck it under the seat, on the metal frame so it would come off easily.

At John's house the man knocked on the front door. John stood beside the man as his mother opened the door.

'Hello, Mrs. Cleary? Is this your son? We found him. He'd got himself lost in Calderstones Park, and he was a little upset.'

John stood there for a few seconds. He said thanks and ran into the house and upstairs to his bedroom. He didn't want to be hit in front of the man and his wife.

His mother never came upstairs afterwards so he didn't know what would happen when he went downstairs. When he eventually did, his mother never did anything; she never hit him or even shouted at him, or mentioned it. It was like it had never happened. He didn't find out what the man had said to his mother. He wasn't too sure if Kevin Dunleavy had told his mother that he'd left them and gone off on his own. So maybe she never knew that he'd been lost in the first place. John never asked. He remembered the man had a beard and glasses; he guessed he might have been a beatnik or something like that, but John still thought he was nice.

As the bus approached Halewood they saw new houses being built everywhere. Construction workers digging the soil and laying drains, driving dumpers, men fixing roof joists and men below them fitting windows. There seemed to be men at work everywhere, even though it was Saturday afternoon. Wherever John looked there were new houses or they were being built. And more fields than he had ever seen. Everything looked new, even the roads. And then there were the kids. It seemed that there were even more kids than workmen; they were all over the place.

When Mary knocked, Margaret's mother opened the door.

'Nice to see you,' she said. 'Margaret's not back yet. Come in. Come in. Take your shoes off.'

John was shocked. He thought, 'Flippin' 'eck! Take your shoes off. Has she gone soft?'

But Mary simply did as she was told straight away. She balanced on one foot, then the other, as she took her shoes off.

'Isn't it lovely up here, Mary?' Mrs. Clarke said. 'Just like being in the countryside. We should have come up here years ago.'

Mrs. Clarke pointed at John's shoes and said, 'Come on, you as well.'

As he took his shoes off he recalled that his mother had made a point of checking he had put new socks on. His mother had checked his socks not once, but twice before he'd left the house. He stepped into the hall shoeless and felt daft. He looked around. All the walls had been painted magnolia and some small pictures hung on them.

'Isn't it beautiful?' said Mrs. Clarke. 'Good quality, the best you can get. Took me ages to choose, cost a fortune as well, but worth it - well worth it - and we're going to get wallpaper to go with it. Axminister you know, Mary; lovely. Lovely to walk on, isn't it?'

It suddenly dawned on John as he looked down. Carpet. They had taken their shoes off in the street for the sake of Mrs. Clarke's carpet. Mrs. Clarke wore slippers. He looked down at his and Mary's feet and felt his face begin to glow with anger.

'Just put them there,' said Mrs. Clarke, pointing to a corner near the door, 'and I'll show you around.'

Mrs. Clarke gave them a tour of the house, even her bedroom. It was clean and everything was new. There was a back kitchen with cupboards built in, a sink with hot and cold water, a toilet and a bathroom with an airing cupboard. And the garden was big. John thought it would be good for football – if there'd been any grass. But it was just soil. And Mrs. Clarke didn't have any sons, only Margaret. She showed them around telling them how great everything was: the house was great; all the other houses were great; all the fields around the houses were great. She said that you could hear the birds in the morning, and that was great. The shops were great. The neighbours were great. It seemed to John that, every soddin' thing was great. After the tour, Mrs. Clarke made them a pot of tea and they waited for Margaret. They waited over half an hour. As they waited, Mrs. Clarke talked of buying a new television, a new three-piece suite, a radiogram, a bedroom suite, a Hoover and even a washing machine.

'No more going down the wash house for me,' declared Mrs. Clarke, and she laughed.

And then she began on the questions.

'Did you like the new tea service?'

'Did you like the carpets?'

'Did you notice the new shops just being built by the bus stop?'

John was bored soft and he could see Mary was as well. Mrs. Clarke didn't ask about her old neighbours or about her old neighbourhood. She never asked Mary about her leaving school at Easter or her new job – nothing. Through the window, Mrs. Clarke caught sight of Margaret and a new friend coming up the path. Mary cheered up. When Mrs. Clarke opened the door she said, 'Hello Helen, how's your mother? Keeping well, is she?'

Margaret said, 'You go upstairs Helen, I'll be up soon.'

Helen went up the stairs without a glance towards Mary or John.

Mary stepped towards Margaret as if to give her friend a hug, but Margaret said, 'Oh how nice to see you, Mary. Keeping well?' and sat down on the settee next to her mother.

'Oh how nice to see you. Keeping well,' echoed in John's mind and he thought, 'God bless us, what's going on here? She sounds daft.'

Then Margaret talked on and on, just like her mother, except that instead of saying everything was great, Margaret said everything was fab. Her new school was fab. They were going to build a swimming pool next to it, which would be fab. Margaret was staying on at school until she was sixteen; taking exams, which would be fab, and she told Mary she'd got to know lots of girls her age and lots of nice lads, who were fab. They were going to build a fab youth club, but when Mary tried to tell Margaret what her old school friends were up to, it was obvious Margaret wasn't interested.

Mrs. Clarke just beamed with pride as she looked at her daughter.

'And Janet's sister's going to be a nurse, isn't she?' said Mrs. Clarke, 'Tell Mary about your friend Sandra; her dad's a schoolteacher. And what about Jane's dad - he's a boss at Ford's, isn't he? Hey, maybe he'll be able to get your John a job there when he leaves school?'

John gritted his teeth. He stared at Mrs. Clarke. He thought, 'We've been here ages and you haven't even noticed me, never even given me a biscuit with my tea. The only time you've spoken to me is to tell me to get my shoes off and now you want to get me a job in a factory, cheeky sod. I'm not gonna work in a factory, I'm going away to sea, to be a seafarer. Daft cow.'

After twenty minutes it was clear it was time to go. John and Mary still had their coats on. They stood to leave. Mary said to Margaret, 'You'll have to come down to visit us.'

'Oh? No. Thanks, Mary. Couldn't go back there, oh no.'

Mrs. Clarke gave a small laugh.

'That's what I was saying to you before. I know you're only talking about visiting, but I tell you what - I wouldn't move back down there for all the tea in China.'

She sounded as if she really meant it. Helen shouted from upstairs.

'I'll have to go up now,' said Margaret. 'I'm learning French and Helen's helping me. We'll probably be doing it for our exams. They don't do French in Saint Pat's, do they? That's a shame that, because it's really fab.'

John looked at Margaret. He thought, 'Bleedin' liar. French, she's joking.' But he felt sorry for his sister.

Margaret went upstairs without waiting to see them off while John stared at their shoes that stood alone in the corner where they'd put them an hour before. As they put them back on John looked at Mary, certain she must also have noticed that Margaret and Helen had kept their shoes on.

As soon as they were out of the house Mrs. Clarke closed the door. She didn't even walk them to the gate and she didn't wave them off. John knew that it was all wrong and he wanted to speak to his sister but he didn't know what to say. He wanted to call Mrs. Clarke and Margaret all the sods and divvies and daft gets under the sun. But he knew Mary felt embarrassed, and calling them names would have made her feel worse.

They waited for ages at the bus stop and still Mary hadn't spoken. John didn't know what to do or say, so he asked a passing woman the time of the next bus.

'They run every half-hour, son.'

'Did you hear that, Mer? Every half-hour! They've got new houses here but the buses are last. Every five minutes round our way, isn't it Mer?'

Mary gave a small smile.

'You know what Uncle Jim would say?' said John. 'He'd say, "The buses here aren't worth a carrot, not worth a carrot". Or he'd say, "The buses here aren't worth a blow on a ragman's trumpet".'

Mary gave what passed for a smile and looked across the road. John wanted her to think of something else, not of Margaret.

He thought back to the times when he was small and his mother would shout at him for annoying her, or what it felt like if he'd had a fight with a kid in the street and hadn't won. Mary would talk to him, put her arm around him and make him laugh – cheer him up. He remembered the times when he was little and used to sleep in her bed and she'd sing him songs. His favourite song was 'Golden Slumbers'. Mary had a good voice; she used to be in the school choir; she used to sing him to sleep, and now she felt bad and it wasn't fair.

They had to change buses in the city centre again. And because they didn't talk, the ride home seemed to take twice as long. They got off the bus outside Saint Patrick's Church and as they walked away Mary turned, took something out of her pocket and put it in the bin at the bus stop. John thought it was the bus tickets or an empty cigarette packet, but then he realised that it wasn't. It took him a few seconds, but then he knew what Mary had put in the bin and he felt even sorrier for her.

When they arrived home their mother asked if they had had any trouble getting to Halewood, and how Margaret and her mother were settling in, and what it was like where Margaret lived.

Mary just said it was alright, and John said the same.

Chapter Three
SCHOOL

Education is what survives when what has
been learned has been forgotten

B, F, Skinner, *New Scientist*

Maths. The boys had their heads in their exercise books when the headmaster, Mr. O'Boyle, came in to talk to the class teacher, Mr. Jackson. After the conversation Mr. O'Boyle glanced round and spoke to the class.

'Are you doing good work for Mr. Jackson?'

The boys replied as one, 'Yes sir!'

The headmaster scanned the classroom; his gaze fixed upon Andrew Ennis. John returned to his work and tried not to listen. He forced himself to concentrate on his subtractions but it was no good. Mr. O'Boyle spoke as though he wanted the class to hear.

'How's your brother Robert getting on at Saint Edward's, Ennis?'

Andrew Ennis stood up.

'Fine Mr. O'Boyle, sir.'

'Tell him that I was asking about him. He'll go far, your Robert.'

Andrew's brother, Robert, had passed the eleven-plus and had been accepted at one of the top colleges in the city, Saint Edward's. Even though Robert had left Saint Patrick's two years before, the teachers would still ask Andrew about Robert when they were in class.

John would get envious. He knew it was a sin but he couldn't help it. And when he remembered how Robert had cheated him over his stamp collection, he became angry. He wanted to say, 'How's Robert getting on? I'll tell you how. He's a friggin' cheat. That's how he's gettin' on!'

John had a large stamp collection and Robert had persuaded John to swap his collection for Robert's collection, plus Robert's spare stamp album and five shillings. Robert had almost begged him. So John had swapped.

A week later John had found out that Robert had noticed a valuable Russian stamp in John's collection. The day after the swap, Robert had gone to a stamp shop in the city centre and sold the Russian stamp for three pounds. The bastard, John thought to himself as he sat in the classroom and remembered. He knew it was swearing but to John, Robert was one. Robert bragged to John about what he had done and laughed. He wanted to punch Robert right in the soddin' mouth. At the time John had thought if that's what you do when you become clever and go to college, I think I'd rather stay with my mates. John hadn't told anyone at home but he knew what Uncle Jim would have said. He'd say, 'I wouldn't piss on him if he was on fire.'

John knew it wasn't a nice thing to say but that's what he thought about Robert Ennis.

At one o'clock John stood in the playground with a group of classmates. They talked about how lucky they were that The Beatles were coming to Liverpool on a Holy Day of Obligation when the school would be closed. They were so engrossed in their conversation about the Northern Premiere of *A Hard Day's Night* that they never noticed Mr. Coffee come into the playground. All they heard was the whistle being blown for the end of dinner time. The boys stopped talking. Mr. Coffee blew the whistle a second time and the boys formed single-file lines. Then he shouted out, 'Right 4A! Ciggy check! You know the drill. Any boy who's been having a sly ciggy at dinnertime won't get past me!'

Mr. Coffee stood erect as the boys filed towards him. Then, as each boy passed him, he bent down, smelt their breath, and shouted out.

'Beans on toast, Mooney. Next!'

'Tomato soup, Edwards. Next!'

'Fish and chips, Farrell. Next!'

A small skinny lad, Tony Connelly, was the next in line but he wouldn't move. The lad behind gave him a shove. Everyone looked at Connelly. Connelly smoked. He walked slowly, head down and stopped a couple of feet away.

'Closer, Connelly!' shouted Mr. Coffee. 'I won't bite.' Connelly took a small step closer, then another. Mr. Coffee bent his head.

'Breathe.'

Connelly lowered his head as he did so. Mr. Coffee grabbed him by the chin.

'Breathe!' he shouted into Connelly's face. His voice echoed around the playground. He seemed to be enjoying it.

'Ciggies, Connelly! I smell the dreaded weed.' Mr. Coffee turned slightly and raised his hand. He slapped Connelly across the face. Connelly stumbled backwards.

'Stay where you are, lad,' Mr. Coffee shouted. He took a step forward, grabbed Connelly by the lapel of his coat and slapped him again and again. John turned away and concentrated on the back of the head of the lad in front, but he could still hear Connelly being slapped.

During the lesson John watched Mr. Jackson as he sat with the group nearest the classroom door. John's group would be next. At the beginning of term Mr. Jackson had explained to class how clouds were formed and why it rained, about how certain rocks were formed over millions of years, how sandstone was created and why there was clay. He gave lessons on how rivers formed and why some places made good ports and why canals were built in certain ways.

One lesson, Mr. Jackson informed the class that they were going to start a project. John liked the sound of it. The class was split up into four groups of six. The project was on the docks, the ships and the cargoes that the ships brought in. John's group was given the task of finding out about the shipping lines. As they chatted in their group about how they would find out about the lines, it felt to John as if they had their own gangs in the class and could talk as much as they wanted to, in their own group. He enjoyed it; it was good.

As the project progressed, one group found books from the local library and asked their dads and uncles about goods that passed through the port. They collected pictures from magazines and newspapers of the different fruits and food that came in on the ships. They made drawings of trees, showing the different types of timber that were imported. Photographs of sheep and cows were matched against pictures of meat and butter and wool.

Another group drew a map of the countries that sent the cargoes and found out about the main ports and the capital cities, and they found out what language was spoken in each country. John's group discovered the names of all the shipping lines that came to Liverpool. There was the Lampart and Holt Line, the Ellerman and Papaganni Line, the Palm Line, the Hall Line, the Blue Funnel Line, the Canadian Pacific Steamship, the Bibby Line and the Elder Dempster line.

John knew that his dad did a lot of work for the Elder Dempster line, and that he and the men who unloaded the Elder Dempster ships called the line the "monkey" because the seafarers on the ship always played tricks on each other, and because some of the crew brought monkeys back from the west coast of Africa. They used the monkeys instead of cats on the ship and sold them when they docked.

John recalled when Peter first went to work on the dock and came home early with Uncle Jim. John had finished school and they all sat at the kitchen table; the conversation concerned parrots. Uncle Jim had told how seafarers would make some money, selling parrots when the ship docked in Liverpool. Uncle Jim said that the men had to be careful trying to get them past the Customs Officer on the dock. The parrots needed to be hidden. He told Peter if the Customs Officer found a parrot on the seafarer, they would be in serious trouble. To get past the Customs Officer they would get the parrots drunk. John could see that Peter wasn't too sure if Uncle Jim was pulling his leg. He said that the night before the ship would dock, the men on board would give the parrot an orange that had been soaked in rum. It would eat the orange, get drunk, and after a few hours would fall asleep. Peter looked at his uncle, still not too sure if he was telling the truth.

Uncle Jim had continued, 'The ship docks in the morning and the parrot we gave the rum soaked orange is dead to the world, out like a light, dreaming about being back in the jungle. My mate Matty Delaney puts the parrot down the front of his kecks head first; you can't see nothing, just a bit of a bulge in the front of his trousers. We're walking towards the gate, past the customs office, and what happens? The parrot starts to wake up. So think of this, the parrot waking up, upside down, pitch black with its head feeling like someone's playing the bongos on it, next to a smelly pair of skivvies. Then it thinks, well it's not all bad; look at the size of that worm. I'll tell you what, Roger Bannister's four-minute mile, that fella wouldn't have had a chance against Matty Delaney. Three minutes, maybe even two an' half that day. Fifty customs officers couldn't have stopped him. Don't even think a copper on a motor bike could have.'

John's class worked on the project for eight weeks. Their final task was to draw pictures of the flags and the funnels of the shipping lines, colour them in and pin them on the classroom walls. When the project was almost finished, John felt very proud. There were pictures of all the cargoes, and magazine and newspaper photographs of dozens of different ships. There were lists and drawings of all the types of ships, general cargoes, refrigerators, bulk carriers and oil tankers. And there was a map with all the different coloured strands radiating out from the port.

For the last two lessons Mr. Jackson had asked the boys to bring in anything they had in their house, or that they could borrow which had something to do with the countries in the project, or the docks, the intention being to display what was brought in to other classes.

On the Monday John brought in the maracas. The boys formed a line and placed the items on a table at the front of the classroom. The amount of items surprised Mr. Jackson and he had to pull out another two desks to accommodate the collection.

John had brought the maracas in on Monday, but he still wanted to bring something else in on Wednesday. On the Tuesday night his dad and Peter had come home with some leaflets from work which contained a few pictures of the docks. John wanted to bring them into class the next day for the project. He knew he should have asked if they needed the leaflets, but if he had, they might have said no, so he took them without asking.

Now he was in the class with the leaflets in his coat pocket. Mr. Jackson stood up as the classroom door opened. It was the new trainee teacher, Mr. Roberts, who had begun his teaching practice at the school a few weeks before. Like Mr. Jackson, he was young. Mr. Roberts always wore a cravat and a blazer with a badge on the breast pocket. The two men talked between themselves for a few minutes, then Mr. Jackson looked at his watch.

'Right 4A. Stop there! Playtime. Make your way out. Quietly! Don't scrape your chairs when you stand up.'

In the schoolyard, Mr. Jackson was on playtime duty. John wanted to take the leaflets over but there was always a group of boys hanging around him. He waited, but Mr. Roberts came into the playground and went over to Mr. Jackson. They spoke to the boys around them and they moved off. John went over.

'Mr. Jackson, I've got some stuff here on the docks, for the project.' There were four separate leaflets. Mr. Jackson looked at the first leaflet and glanced at the others. He passed two to Mr. Roberts. They took their time reading. John stood there like a prune. As he waited, he called himself for not reading the leaflets first. He thought it was boring stuff to do with dock work, but the photographs of the ships and the cranes on the leaflets would be useful for the project.

Mr. Roberts laughed and spoke to Mr. Jackson.

'Listen to this, Lawrence: "The Blue Union's view is that only by showing a united front can we hope to achieve changes that benefit not just the bosses but all those working on the docks. Solidarity, not Division; only through struggle has the working man ever achieved anything, and only through a collective struggle now can we win through." Oh, man the barricade, comrade.' He laughed again.

'What about this,' said Mr. Jackson: ''The Transport and General talks of democracy, but where was the democracy when the National Amalgamated Stevedores and Dockers were expelled from the TUC in 1959? This is capitalist democracy; just a tool that changes to suit those in power and those who keep them there. What we need is real democracy - true representation by the workers, for the workers.'' Sounds like someone's upset.' They both burst out laughing.

Mr. Roberts passed the leaflets to Mr. Jackson, who passed them back to John. Mr. Roberts giggled like a girl. He tried to stop and put his hand to his mouth, but he couldn't. Neither teacher looked at John; they simply turned round and walked away. John felt awful; he felt last; he felt like shite.

At first he was angry with himself for not having read the leaflets, not trying to understand what was in them. But he thought, 'No, it's not my fault; it's them. They're soddin' ignorant. Who the soddin' hell do they think they are? I wish I was bigger, I just wish I was, I'd give them such a bloody good dig. Or better still, take that stupid-looking cravat off Mr. Roberts and strangle the pair of bastards with it.'

The class finished the project that day and John was glad. All he could think of during the lesson was that he hoped Mr. Jackson didn't ask him anything because he would have told him to fuck off. After school he carried his maracas home. He'd picked them off the display table without asking for permission. He'd just taken them, half wishing Mr. Jackson would notice him and say something. As he walked home he considered mentioning what had happened to his mother or dad, but he knew he wouldn't. He knew what they would say.

'Well the teacher must be right; he's a teacher, isn't he?'

'They're the teachers; if they don't want the leaflets it's up to them.'

Mary wouldn't be interested. He could say something to Peter, but he hadn't been working down the docks long and John thought he might have embarrassed him. He would have liked to have told Uncle Jim but he was scared his uncle might go up to the school and cause murder. So when he got home he said nothing.

Chapter Four
CHURCH

By the 1890s Liverpool was the largest Roman Catholic diocese in England with over 400,000 people, one-fifth of the total Catholic population.

T, Gallagher, *The Irish in the Victorian City*

As usual, on the day before a Holy Day of Obligation and before the last lesson, the teachers shepherded their classes to the Church for confession.

John finished his penance while the three priests in their confessional boxes listened, or waited to listen to and absolve the sins of half the pupils at John's school.

A boy stood outside each confessional even though they all knew that they shouldn't wait there, because sometimes the priest could be heard shouting. And sometimes the boy standing outside would hear a lot more than shouting. But if he didn't wait directly outside, if he waited in the pew, when it was his turn a boy from another pew might run out and get in to the confessional box first. So they waited their turn near the door. Some even joked and put their ears to the door for the benefit of their mates. But this was dangerous because not only might a teacher see them, but it made them fair game for the next boy to do the same to them.

John looked towards the main altar. The main altar area extended to both vestry doors. The area and altar rail were curved to accommodate the bottom step of the first of the dozen curved steps to the platform where the pulpit stood. Six more steps continued, leading towards the tabernacle and altar itself. At the sides were benches for the altar boys and behind the altar there was a large mural of the crucifixion. John stared at the bottom of the cross where the Virgin Mary and Apostles stood along with Roman soldiers who knelt, throwing dice and gambling for the clothes of Jesus, while one soldier held a vinegar-soaked sponge on the end of a spear.

His mother wanted him to serve on the altar but he was concerned as to how well he'd carry out his duties with a packed congregation looking on. At ten o'clock mass on Sundays the Church was filled with hundreds of parishioners. The elevated altar meant that all those attending mass were able see everything that went on during the service. If an altar boy were to drop something or pass the priest the wrong book, it would be embarrassing. Or worse, if the altar boy tripped over his cassock and fell down the steps, it'd be terrible. John thought the boy wouldn't want to go on the altar again if he'd done that, no chance.

He told Mike about his intention to be an altar boy but Mike didn't want to know. John led Mike to believe that John's mother was making him serve on the altar. He also told Mike that altar boys received money for going with the priest on the monthly visit to parishioners' houses of a Friday night, the altar boy's job being to inform the parishioners that the priest was due. The priest would give the altar boys a shilling, or sometimes two, from the donations collected. John told Mike that he was only doing it for the money. Although he knew he was lying, he considered it a white lie and one that helped the Church, so it was alright. He told Mike that he was going to save up and buy a case ball. But Mike wasn't impressed and told John, 'I'm not going around the streets with the priest dressed up in all that altar gear, not even for a pound!'

John felt a bit sorry for him. He knew Mike could be a bit slow at times. Mike believed the altar boys went around the parish in their cassock and cotter. When he told him they never, Mike became upset. John accepted that it wasn't Mike's fault because the priest never came around to New Harrington Street due to the street being on the dividing line between two parishes: the priests in Saint Patrick's believed it was in Saint Malachy's parish and the priests in Saint Malachy's believed it was in Saint Patrick's.

It was due to the priests carrying out the monthly rounds that his uncle sometimes called into John's house on a Friday night. When Uncle Jim knew there was a visit from his own parish priest, he would go the pub from work and then to his sister's for his tea. John's mother knew this. Sometimes she didn't say anything and sometimes she did; most times she didn't. Unless they started to argue, then it would be, 'Why have you come here tonight? I know, because the priest's coming to yours; you're a big man, aren't you? Can't face the priest. I know, I've been told; hide in the toilet if the priest comes; won't come out till he's gone; big man, you, James Mulhearn.'

Uncle Jim wasn't too bothered. John didn't think Uncle Jim liked arguing on Friday nights if he could help it. But he might make a reply that his sister wouldn't hear. He once asked John what he had done that day at school. And John had told him; the class had had a lesson on the Catechism.

'Who made you?'

'God made me.'

'Why did God make you?'

'God made me to know him, love him and serve him in this world and to be happy with him forever in the next.'

'Oh I know that one, but the one I learnt was a bit different. Why did God make me? God made me to go out to work and get some money, to put on the plate so the priest could go out with his mates for a bevvy.'

John's dad had been there at the time and had laughed, but only because John's mother was upstairs. John thought that was Uncle Jim's way of arguing back on a Friday night.

*   *   *

John knelt in front of the television.

'John, close your mouth,' his mother said. 'It looks like you're catching flies.'

He glanced at her, then back at the television. The Beatles had stepped off a plane. They were holding their flight bags and they waved to the crowds of screaming fans. The reporter talked about their recent Australian tour and their visit to America. John stared at the television. He moved even closer to it. The reporter spoke about the feature film The Beatles had just completed, and of their arrival in Liverpool the following day.

'Tomorrow, mam, did you hear the man on the telly? They're coming tomorrow.'

'Yes, John. I heard.'

When John heard his dad and Uncle Jim come in, he went upstairs to his room. He stared at his collection of Beatles pictures on the wall. He went to the wardrobe and took out Peter's black jacket. It was too small for Peter now; it was being kept for John. He tried it on in front of the mirror, but it was still too big. His fingertips stuck out just below the sleeves. He turned the collar inside to make it look like a Beatle jacket, combed his fringe down and checked himself in the mirror again. He pretended to play a guitar and sang a Beatle song, then he jumped onto the bed. He bounced as he sang and played the "guitar" with his eyes screwed shut.

He was on stage. There were thousands in the audience. They screamed while he played the guitar. When he looked around, The Beatles were behind him, playing. He turned to the crowd and sang at the top of his voice. In the audience, Mike stood at the front of the crowd, Steve next to him, the Dunleavys behind them and Steve waved an autograph book and pointed at it. The fans shouted his name so John played his "guitar" faster. The crowd shouted louder.

'John! John! John!'

The crowd shouted louder.

'JOHN!'

In mid-bounce John opened his eyes. It was his mother calling him. No fans. No Beatles. No guitar.

'John, what are you doing? We thought the ceiling was coming through.'

John dropped his hands from the imaginary guitar.

'Your tea's ready,' said his mother. 'And what are you doing with Peter's jacket on? Take it off.' She studied him for a second. 'And comb your hair…you look daft.'

John heard his Uncle Jim speaking as he made his way from down the stairs. He stopped to listen; the side of the stairs had been covered in hardboard, so he could not be seen, but nothing of interest was being talked about so he carried on walking.

'John, wash your hands,' said his mother.

'Hello lad,' said Uncle Jim when he got downstairs.

'Hiya,' said John.

He went to the sink, and his dad and Uncle Jim carried on talking.

'A different government's going to help though, isn't it Jim?' said John's dad. 'They've got to be better.'

'We'll see. They can't be worse. Wouldn't hold out too much hope if they're anything like this lot 'round here.' said Uncle Jim.

'What d'you mean?'

'Y'know, the councillors around here take more notice of the parish priest than they do of the likes of you or me. You've got the priest telling the people how to vote half the time.'

'That's not so,' said John's mother.

'Kathleen, it is. If the priest likes the councillor, if the councillor goes to Church and all that, then the word's put out to vote for him. Not that it matters that much for getting elected in these wards, but they like to have the priest's blessing; it makes it easier for them. I wouldn't be surprised if the full-time Labour Officials have a word with the parish priest beforehand about the bloke's that's standing.'

John dried his hands and sat at the table.

'Ah, you're talking daft now, Jim,' said his dad.

'Am I? Look at Muldoon the Councillor.'

'Good man, him,' said John's mother. 'Always see him in Church.'

'Good man! He's as bent as a nine bob note. If you gave him dropsy and slipped him a few quid he'd get it so you moved up on the housing list. Given a new house before you were due one. Bent!'

'Never; good, God fearing man; good Catholic.'

'You know what, Kathleen? If they found out that Jack the Ripper was a Catholic, you'd say, "Good man him, always went to Holy Communion."'

'The councillors are not all bad, Jim,' said John's dad.

John's mother laid the plates on the table

'A lot of them are, Tom. Listen to this. You know the people around here, the Labour Party could put a monkey up at election time and it would get in. The councillors don't have to do nothing to get the people to vote for them, just be well thought of by the Church. Well this is what I'm getting to; this'll kill you. Last year I was having a few pints up Park Road.'

'That's not like you, Jim Mulhearn,' said John's mother

'Alright, alright Kathleen, you aren't listening to what I'm gonna tell you. Just listen, you might learn something. Anyway, Jack Muldoon comes in the pub with a few of his cronies. So we let on to each other, then I thought, I'll try something here, just for a laugh, just to see what happens. I went over and said, "Alright Jack, can I have a word with you?" Probably thought I was going to put the bite on him, ask him to get me a new house or get a mate of mine a job with the council. So he says, "Yeah sure, let's go over there in the corner. I says, "What it is, Jack, I'm thinking of joining the Labour Party." He went the colour of boiled shite.'

'Language,' said John's mother.

She dropped the knives and forks on the table and looked at her brother.

Uncle Jim continued "But you're - you're, you're -"
'Muldoon couldn't get his words out - "you're with the other crowd, aren't ya? You can't," he said. You should have seen the look on his face; you'd think he'd seen a ghost. So I said,' "No, I'm going to tear my Party card up. I've been thinking about it for a while now; I'm packing them in. I want to come with youse in the Labour Party."

'Do you know what he said? "Oh, er, sorry, er, Jim. I just remembered we're full up. Our ward's full up - can't take no more." Full up! Full up! Have you ever heard the likes? Bleedin' full up! I know for a fact, because I have a bevvy with the fella that serves behind the bar where they have their monthly meetings, only two or three turn up. They could meet in a soddin' telephone box. Full up! I'll show my arse in Woolworth's window if they're full up. Then he wanted to buy me a pint, said I should try again next year. Try again next year, like as though I was going for a job, cheeky get.'

John's mother held a dish of cottage pie; she banged it down on the table.

'I won't tell you again; language. And anyway, what's that got to do with the Church?'

'Everything. The Church are giving the OK if the councillor wants to be bent, so long as he's a Catholic and does the Church a few favours. Look at the new Cathedral that's getting built in town; that's the councillors and the Church again.'

'Nothing wrong with a Cathedral getting built, surely Jim?' said John's dad.

'There's something wrong when the land it's getting built on should have went to build decent houses in the Thirties.'

'What do you mean?'

'What do I mean, Tom! I'll tell you, that land should have gone to build better homes for the people. There's enough bad houses around here now; I don't have to tell you what it was like before the war - diabolical! They weren't supposed to sell council property to private firms or concerns, like the Church - that went

48

against Labour National Party policy - but this is Liverpool. This is where the good old Catholic Church rules.'

'You're not making sense!' declared John's mother. She moved back to the cooker and brought two pans to the table.

'Aren't I, Kathleen?' replied Uncle Jim. 'Well, I think I am. The councillors, who wanted to sell the land to the Church, deprived ordinary people of a chance of better houses. The councillors who weren't in the Church's pocket threw the right-wing councillors out of the council. Then lo and behold, the Labour party full-time officials in London came up and reinstated them all and everything's rosy again. Councillors get their jobs and perks back. Church gets its land. People get no houses. Great, innit.'

John's mother held the pans until her brother had finished then put them down. There were cabbage and peas in them. She bent her head towards her brother.

'Is that the kind of nonsense you lot talk about in the Star Club? Load of baloney, all that what you just said.'

'Kath, I know you don't rate me much because I like a pint, fair enough, but that doesn't make it wrong what I'm saying.'

'No! No, you've lost your faith Jim Mulhearn, that's your problem. You're not a Catholic any more; you've told me, not even a Christian.'

'Nothing wrong with believing in Christ if you want to. The *real* word of Christ. It's the ones that go around calling themselves Christians, that's when the trouble starts. Especially, those that call themselves good Christians, they're the worst.'

'You're talking rubbish.' John's mother sat down.

'Look at Kennedy; he was hand in glove with the Church over there.'

'Oh, no, no, no, won't have a word said against that man, not in this house, and his poor wife and children; terrible that, terrible. That was a communist that done that as well.'

'Load of rubbish; never a communist, that fella who shot Kennedy. Stinks, all that.'

'He was a good man him, Kennedy; good Catholic.'

'What about his old fella? Was he a good Catholic? Bootlegger, rumrunner, carrying on with all kinds of women, mate of Hitler's?'

'No no that's not true; you just make things up you, Jim Mulhearn.'

'Kathleen, it is true, but you won't read about it in the Catholic Pic. That's your problem; you believe everything the papers tell ya. You're like a pawnshop; you take anything in.'

'I've got a mind of my own. I can decide what's what in the papers.'

'Kathleen, half of what you read in the papers is lies and the other half's shite.'

'That's enough of talk like that, Jim Mulhearn,' shouted John's mother.

No one spoke for a while, then John's mother spooned the cottage pie onto the plates.

'So you're going to see The Beatles tomorrow?' asked Uncle Jim.

Before John had a chance to answer his mother spoke.

'I haven't said he can go yet.'

'Mam!'

'I want to see who he's going with first.'

'Mam, I'm not a kid; you said I could go.' John was going to say something else when his dad spoke to him.

'So do you know all their names?' asked his uncle

'Yeah, of course I do, and I know what they do in the group. George is the guitar player. Paul's the singer. Ringo's the drummer. And, John's...the leader. They all have different jobs. But they all work together.'

Uncle Jim pointed his fork at John's dad.

'That's what I was saying before, Tom, unity is strength. Everyone's got to stick together. I'll explain in more detail when I take you for a pint after.'

'Jim, Jim, Jim,' said John's dad, each word slowly dragged out wearily.

Chapter Five
WISHING

To the ordinary working man, the sort you would meet in
any pub on a Saturday night, Socialism does not mean
much more that better wages and shorter hours and
nobody bossing you about.

George Orwell, *The Road to Wigan Pier*

John and Mike arrived at Princes Road and stood together
on the edge of the kerb. The crowd leaned out to see The Beatles.
There were no cars on the road but suddenly there was a buzz of
whispers and passed-on messages. They were coming.

Fans leaned out into the road; in the distance the cars could
be seen. The crowd near the cars waved as they passed; some tried
to reach out and touch them. The sun gleamed off the black,
polished paintwork. The talk turned into cheers as the cars came
closer. When the first car drew near it slowed down and stopped.
The noise from the crowd stopped as well and all John could hear
was the sound of the cars' engines idling. The rear window of the
first car wound down. The passenger looked out and pointed to
where the boys stood. Mike spoke quietly, 'Look! He's pointing at
you, John!'

John noticed his reflection in the car door. He saw a large
smile which disappeared as the car door opened.

'Do you want a ride?' asked the man inside.

Mike leaned towards him. He whispered, 'Go on,' and
nudged John forwards, 'Go on, John,' he said. 'I would.'

'Are you coming?'

'He wants you to go John,' said Mike, 'because you've got the same name as him, maybe. Go on.'

John stepped off the kerb and into the car. When he sat down the car pulled away. He didn't know what to say but when he looked up John Lennon smiled down at him and asked him a question.

'Where d'you live?'

'Down the grid.'

'What number?'

'Cucumber.'

'What's your name?'

'Mary Jane.'

They both laughed and, as the sun appeared from behind the clouds, John turned towards it, closed his eyes and faced the light.

*   *   *

John Cleary opened first one eye then the other. Then he turned away from the morning sunlight that streamed through his bedroom window and tried to recapture the voice from his dream.

'Where d'you live?'

'Down the grid.'

'It's a kids' saying, that one.'

'The things you say when you're a kid.'

But other voices from downstairs interrupted the voices in his head and someone climbed the stairs. As John got out of bed the voices from his dream disappeared and the sounds of his family took over.

As he went down the stairs he saw Uncle Jim's coat hung on the back door. His mother was at the sink. Peter sat to one side of Uncle Jim.

Uncle Jim looked up, 'Hello, lad,' he said.

'Hiya.'

Peter turned around and winked. His mother looked up.

'You're up early.'

'Couldn't sleep.'

She turned to her brother, 'That's you, that!'

'What's me? What do you mean?'

'Making me shout. You've woken the lad up now.'

John wanted to go back upstairs. But instead he said, 'I was awake before that, Uncle Jim; you never woke me up... or my mam.'

'There y'are, Kath. I never woke the lad up,' said Uncle Jim, and he smiled at John.

John sat at the table. He saw Uncle Jim's boots under the armchair.

'Do you want a cup of tea?' asked Uncle Jim. 'There's some fresh made in the pot.' He smiled and raised his eyebrows, then nodded his head to the teapot. There was a plate of toast next to it.

'No thanks,' said John.

'What about some breakfast?' his mother asked. 'Do you fancy some cornflakes or toast? I'll make some fresh toast.'

'No. After, maybe.'

John knew they were being nice because they'd been arguing. It was always the same.

His dad came through the back door. He carried a newspaper.

'You took your time,' said John's mother.

John's dad gave a small cough and lowered his head slightly. He looked at Uncle Jim, then at John.

'Alright, son,' he said. 'Up nice and early.' He sat down facing Uncle Jim.

'Excited, isn't he?' said Peter. 'Going with all his mates to see The Beatles this afternoon. Can't wait, can he? Wants to be front of the queue.'

'Won't be a queue,' said John. 'I'm not going to see Father Christmas at the grotto. It'll be a crowd.'

'You're right. Too old for the grotto now, aren't you? Hey, think of all them girls in the crowd. Might see someone you fancy.'

John lowered his head.

'I wonder if the crowds will be like ours at work in the pen, Uncle Jim?' said Peter.

'Yeah,' said Uncle Jim. 'Only them kids today will be up there pushing and shoving each other because they want to be there. We don't have any bleedin' choice.'

'Less of that talk, Jim Mulhearn,' said John's mother. 'Anyway, I didn't say he could go yet. I want to see who he's going with first and have a word with them.'

'Mam,' said John. 'I told you yesterday who I was going with.'

'I want to see who you're going with before you go.'

'Ah, hey mam!'

John's mother dried her hands, sat in the armchair and read a woman's magazine. Peter read his dad's paper.

'How do you think it'll go today, Jim?' asked John's dad.

'Hard to say, Tom. Depends how strong the men feel about it. If they feel strong enough about it we'll be OK. If the Harbour Board wants to argue the toss then we'll have to hit the cobbles. At the end of the day we're down there to put food on the table, not to take any nonsense from that shower. If the lads stick together it'll be alright.'

'Don't you ever do any work down there?' said John's mother. 'Do you just argue all day? It's a wonder you ever get time to unload them ships with all the meetings you have.'

'Unloaded one last week, Kath,' said Uncle Jim, turning to face his sister. 'Cold ship, a fridge ship, brought you a lovely shoulder of New Zealand lamb, but you didn't... '

'I don't want knock-off stuff in this house. You should go to confession you, Jim Mulhearn.' She looked at her brother as she rolled the magazine up.

'Wasn't knock-off Kath, just damaged. That's all; damaged goods. Sling broke. A few shoulders of lamb fell out. Got a bit dirty on the quay. They couldn't put them back, couldn't sell them. A bit scraped, that's all.'

'Don't believe you.'

Uncle Jim unfolded his arms and put his head in his hands. He stared straight ahead at John's dad and shook his head once. John's mother never stopped looking at her brother as she tapped the rolled-up magazine on the side of her leg. John remembered a teacher at school who would roll his newspaper up before using it to hit the children over their heads. His mother did the same to him.

Uncle Jim looked at his sister. 'It's one of the perks of the job, getting stuff like that,' he said.

'That's not true, that,' said John's mother, pointing the magazine at her brother as she spoke. 'Robbed. Knock-off. It was knock-off.'

'Kath, it wasn't... '

'Jim!' interrupted John's dad. 'About the meeting this morning.'

'Oh yeah,' said Uncle Jim, turning round. 'You'll be alright. No problem.' He folded his arms again. 'Just got to stick together, that's all.'

Mary called from the bedroom, 'Mam can you come up a sec?'

John's mother left the kitchen. Uncle Jim watched her go to the stairs, then moved his gaze along the hardboard in line with his sister's footsteps. When he heard her go into the bedroom and close the door he spoke again.

'Yeah, well I... '

'Clark Gable was saying,' said Peter, 'that... '

'Who?' said Uncle Jim.

'Clark Gable, he works in Timmy Reynolds gang. He... '

'They don't call him Clark Gable! It's Ben Gable.'

'They call him Clark Gable, I'm sure.' Peter picked up a cup of tea. 'He's got a pencil thin moustache?'

'Yeah.' said Uncle Jim and his ears stick out?'

'That's right.'

'Yeah.'

'And he lives alone with his mam.'volunteered Peter

'Yeah, and he thinks he's a smart fella with the women; Jack-the-lad.'

'Yeah, Clark Gable,' said Peter triumphantly.

'No!' Uncle Jim spoke as though he was speaking to a child. 'He's got cross-eyes as well like Ben Turpin. You know who Ben Turpin is?'

'The comedian from the silent pictures,' said Peter

'Well the fella you're talking about thinks he's Clark Gable but he looks like Ben Turpin, so the lads call him Ben Gable.'

'Go 'way - is that it?' said Peter, and gave a small laugh. His dad took the paper back. John's mother came in. They hadn't heard her as she came down the stairs.

'What's so funny?' she asked.

'Nothing, nothing, Kath,' said Uncle Jim. He picked a piece of toast off the plate, 'Any marmalade?'

John's mother went to the table and felt the teapot, then sat down and picked up the magazine again. 'In the larder.'

Uncle Jim went to the larder. He reached over John's dad to open the glass doors at the top. He opened them, then shut them and opened the pull-down door below. John's dad had to lean forward over the table.

'At the back,' said his sister, 'It's bad for your teeth, that.'

Uncle Jim turned around. He held a jar of marmalade.

'Then why'd you get it?'

'For the lad,' she pointed at John. 'He brushes his teeth; I make him.'

'Well if I knew I was having marmalade this morning, Kath, I would have brought my toothbrush.'

'Yes well, you should be home with your toothbrush. That's where you should be.'

'If I'd known last night when I went out that I'd be spending the night on your couch, Kath, I would have put it in my top pocket.'

'Jim,' said John's dad, still leaning forward, 'are you having that marmalade or what?'

'Nar, bad for your teeth and I've got no toothbrush, so I'm stitched.' He put the jar back inside and closed the pull-down door. 'If I'd had my toothbrush with me at the club last night, the lads in the card school would have thought I'd come to clean them out.'

Peter laughed. His dad continued to try to read his paper. Uncle Jim picked up a piece of toast and turned to his sister.

'Listen Kath, I only wanted some marmalade on my toast.' He held the toast up. 'Not a lecture on the state of my teeth. I know, what about some bacon instead?'

John's mother put her magazine down and stared hard at the television set. He glanced at his mother's frozen stare in the reflection of the dead screen.

'No,' his mother spoke. 'I've got none; it's for tomorrow.'

'You've got none, it's for tomorrow?' said Uncle Jim.

'Yes; clean your ears out, or don't you understand the Queen's English?'

'Just one slice?'

'You can't have any.' She picked up the magazine. 'You know why.'

Uncle Jim looked at John's dad but he was reading his paper, or making an effort to. Uncle Jim looked at Peter and shrugged. Uncle Jim didn't know. Peter tried to tell him; he mouthed why. Uncle Jim didn't get it; he shook his head and put his hand to his ear. Peter tried again, but his mother's magazine went down.

'What's going on?'

'Nothing, nothing. Why?' asked Peter.

She looked at Peter. Uncle Jim turned to face her and gave her a soft, false smile, looking like a docker's version of Stan Laurel. His sister glared at him and then at Peter. She stood up and went to the stairs. She turned and looked at her brother, who produced a soft smile again. John's mother went up the stairs.

No one spoke until the bedroom door clicked shut. Then Uncle Jim spoke to John.

'Stand there, son,' he pointed to the bottom of the stairs. 'Go on, quick.'

John stood where he was told. His dad's and Peter's eyes were glued on Uncle Jim as he went to the larder.

'Bacon, bacon, bacon,' Uncle Jim sang and rubbed his hands.

'What are you doing, Jim?' asked John's dad.

'The bacon; obvious, isn't it?' Uncle Jim said as he opened the top doors of the larder and looked in, then closed them and opened the pull-down door. John's dad leant forward again.

'There, there it is!'

'Kath'll kill you,' said John's dad. It's Friday and it's a Holy Day of Obligation.' When he spoke it looked like he was talking to the table.

'Oh yeah, Friday. No meat on Friday; no meat on Holy Day of Obligation you'd think we were back in the Dark Ages.'

He took the bacon out of the wrapping, picked a slice and held it up.

'I'll have this well done and eaten before she comes back down. Just watch me.'

He put the rest of the bacon back in the bag and closed the pull-down door. John's dad straightened up, as Uncle Jim went to the cooker. He put the bacon in the pan and lit the gas. He went back to the larder opened a drawer. John's dad pulled his chair in. Uncle Jim pulled out a knife. John's dad put his hand on the chair and went to move it back out but then Uncle Jim opened the pull-down door so John's dad leaned forward again. As he did, John's dad shook his head and put his hand to his mouth. Uncle Jim held a packet of lard, cut a corner off and went back to the cooker. John's dad reached behind to close the pull-down door of the larder.

Uncle Jim put the lard in the pan, picked up the bacon, stopped and turned around. He pointed upstairs.

'Girls' talk. I've got loads of time. John, don't stand there, er sit, yeah, sit at the bottom of the stairs. A few steps up, that looks better. That's it, and tell me as soon as the bedroom door opens.' He looked at John's dad. 'Just in case.' He held the bacon up with a fork. 'Nice and thick, this.'

John looked at his dad and Peter. Their eyes were glued on the bacon.

Uncle Jim turned towards John.

'First sign of Kath, er your mam, give me the wire. Er, let me know lad.' He put the bacon in the pan, waved the fork in the direction of John, wrinkled his nose and shook his head. 'We won't need him, but you know... ' he spoke to John's dad, 'just in case.'

John's dad mouthed 'We'; his mouth stayed open, his eyes fixed on the bacon.

Uncle Jim pushed the bacon around the pan with the knife; he sang a blues song: 'Born under a bad sign, I've been down since I began to crawl. If it wasn't for bad luck I wouldn't have no luck at all.' He turned around. 'Do you want me to do you a slice, Tom?'

'No no, no,' spluttered John's dad.

'What about you, Peter?' Uncle Jim went to the larder.

'No no, I'm alright,' said Peter.

He continued his trip to the larder. Peter jumped up and his chair nearly tipped over.

'No! I'm alright honest, Uncle Jim!'

Uncle Jim stopped in his tracks.

'It's alright, I'm only getting some bread; what's wrong?' Uncle Jim went to the larder and took out two slices of bread, went back to the cooker and sang again, 'Born under a bad sign, yeah born under a bad sign,' then began to dance. He put his feet together and bent one knee after the other as if he were walking or climbing stairs; he shook his backside and sang some more, 'Born under a bad sign, yeah. Only wine and women is all I crave, big slice of bacon's gonna carry me to my grave, born under a bad sign.'

John felt himself blush. He didn't want to watch so instead turned and looked up the stairs, but he couldn't help himself. He turned back again. His uncle was frying bread to go with his bacon. John's dad didn't look like he was breathing. John heard it before he saw it. The bedroom door opened.

'It's my mam!' cried John.

'What did you say, John?' His mother spoke but she had her back to him.

'Er, er, nothing mam!'

'What are you shouting for?'

'Nothing, nothing.'

John looked at Uncle Jim. Uncle Jim looked at his dad and spoke.

'She's only been up there ten seconds. Soddin' 'ell, the thing's not cooked yet.'

John heard Mary speak. His mother went back in the bedroom and closed the door again.

'She's gone back in,' said John.

'Great!' He looked at John's dad. 'Girls talk.' He pointed to the ceiling with the knife and sang again.

John turned. The sound of his mother's voice was near the bedroom door, then the door opened.

'Right, well, that's what you do, girl,' his mother said to Mary. 'Don't have any messing from them.' She turned and looked down the stairs at John. John froze; he didn't know if it was another false alarm. His mother turned again towards Mary, 'And thanks for telling me about, the other.' His mother came out of the room backwards and closed the door. She turned around and walked down the stairs, then stopped.

'John what are you...?'

John stared at her open-mouthed, and then looked at Uncle Jim, who had turned over a piece of fried bread, unaware that his sister was on the stairs. John looked back at his mother. He shook himself out of his trance.

'Mam!'

'What?'

John looked at Uncle Jim.

'Mam!'

'Mam!' said Uncle Jim.

John's mother came down the stairs.

'John, get up off the stairs, you're in my way. What are you doing sitting on the stairs anyway?'

Uncle Jim tried to pick the bacon out of the pan, 'Oh, oh ouch, soddin' hell!'

His mother's view of her brother was blocked by the boarded up stairway, but she heard him. She called out, 'What did you say, Jim? I hope you're not swearing down there.'

Uncle Jim picked the bacon up with his fingertips. The heat rose and the fat dripped into the pan.

'The back door,' said Peter.

'No she'll see you, coming down the stairs,' said his dad.

'What's going on down there?' asked John's mother. 'John, move out my way lad; I've told you once.'

'The fireplace,' said Peter.

Uncle Jim held the bacon out in front of him like a smelly fish. He got to the fireplace as John's mother came in the room. Uncle Jim had his head lowered. The fire wasn't lit. The grate was empty. It was summer. John's dad groaned. Uncle Jim's head was bowed down towards the grate. He brought his hands up like he was going to join them for prayers.

'Ow!'

'Jim?' said John's mother.

Uncle Jim spun around quick. His hands at his sides closed into fists and he pushed them into his trouser pockets.

'Alright, alright, alright how's it going?' he spoke fast. 'How's it going, you know?' He nodded his head to the ceiling.

No one spoke until John's dad said, 'Girls' talk.'

'Yeah that's it, Uncle Jim smiled. 'Girls' talk, girls' talk. How is it, Kath?'

'Have you been drinking down here when I was up there? Or is it that you're just daft?' She went to the cooker and turned the gas ring off. 'That fried bread's burnt,' she sniffed. 'What's that smell?'

Uncle Jim took his hands out his pockets and wiped one hand on his trouser leg. He bent his knees and put his hands behind him like he was trying to warm them. John watched, fascinated, as his Uncle tried to get heat from an empty fire grate.

'What's that smell? John's mother asked again.

'The bread; it's burnt,' said John's dad, 'you've just said so yourself. Jim fancied some fried bread then forgot about it because he was talking about today's meeting.'

John's mother sniffed a couple of times and went towards the larder.

John's dad stood up in front of her and said, 'I don't know if we'll be working all day or home early.' He looked at Peter. 'Ready, son?'

Uncle Jim sat down on the armchair and put his boots on.

'If you're coming home early you can start wallpapering this room,' said John's mother.

'What?' his dad said. 'We mightn't be living here next month.'

'We will be, don't talk daft. Anyway, it doesn't matter; it needs doing.' John's mother looked at her brother. 'If he's with you, he can give you a hand. Maybe he can help the lad mix some paste.' She looked at her brother. 'He must be useful for something.'

John's dad looked at Uncle Jim, who put his head down and finished tying his bootlaces.

'I've got some rolls of wallpaper I was saving for our bedroom,' continued John's mother. 'They're in the parlour. They'll do for in here.'

'Wallpaper... ' said John's dad. He was about to say more when Peter spoke.

'Come on dad, we'll be late.' Peter took a drink of tea then grabbed his coat off the back of his chair. John had the impression his mother knew something had been going on. She went into the parlour.

'Come on, quick!' said John's dad in a low voice. 'Let's make tracks.' He grabbed Uncle's Jim's coat and passed it to him; his own coat was underneath. 'Peter, get the carrying out, son.' He nodded to the sandwiches on top of the television. John's dad opened the back door then turned around.

'You won't need any of these sarnies, will you Jim?'

'What do you mean?' said Uncle Jim.

'Well, you've got your dinner.' He pointed towards Uncle Jim's trousers. Uncle Jim looked down and gave a false smile.

'Ah, funny fella,' he said.

They all went out. John heard the backyard door open and Peter, then his dad, laughing; the backyard door shut. John went back to his room. Best get out of the way, just in case, he told himself.

*   *   *

When John and his mother came out of nine o'clock Mass his mother didn't talk about the priest's sermon the way she usually did. At the corner of Park Place and Hill Street she stopped to talk to Mrs. Flannery. John went and stood outside Brennans'.

Lots of kids went into Brennans' shop. May and Joe were in their sixties and had lots of patience while they waited for the kids to choose which sweets they wanted. But Brennans' didn't sell *Superman* comics or *DC* or *Marvel*, only the likes of the *Dandy* or *Beano* or *Eagle*. There were no American comics so John had to go to one of the other shops to buy his *Batman* or *Spiderman* comics. They never sold any toys, either. Just sweets, newspapers and cigarettes, snuff and shoe polish. Stuff like that.

When they got back home John's mother set up the ironing board. John buttered a piece of toast, grabbed a comic and sat down at the table.

'I'll be going after dinner, mam. About three o'clock.'

His mother ironed a shirt with her back to him. 'You won't, John.'

'Yeah, today mam, have you forgot? It's not tomorrow, it's today The Beatles are coming.'

'I know when they're coming, John.' His mother carried on ironing. 'But you're not going.'

'What? What? What d'ya mean?'

His mother stopped ironing and turned round. 'It's too far to go, and... '

'It's not too far mam!' John butted in.

'John, don't interrupt me. It's too far and Mary told me this morning that you have to go past where they're building Saint Martin's, where all those gangs have been fighting.'

'Mam, mam we don't have to go that way. We can go another way.'

'John. No. It'll be too dangerous. There'll be thousands up there. Mrs. Flannery was telling me before. She said all police leave has been stopped because of the crowds. She's not letting her Michael go.'

'Mam! Mickey Flannery is only soddin' nine!'

'John don't talk to me like that.'

'Mam I'm not a kid.'

'John. No.'

'It's not friggin' fair!'

'John!'

'It's not friggin' friggin' fair!'

'John! Get to your room.'

Chapter Six
BILLY

He was of the faith chiefly in the sense that the
church he currently did not attend was Catholic.

Kingsly Amis, *One Fat Englishman*

John waited in his room for half an hour. He sat on the floor
with his back against the bed. Then he stood up and looked at the
pictures of The Beatles, then sat down on the edge of the bed. He
tried to think of reasons to give his mother to let him go. But for
every good reason he thought of, he also knew his mother would
come up with a better reason for his not going. And then, without
any planned series of good reasons, he went back downstairs.

His mother had moved the furniture and had begun to strip
the wallpaper. She turned as he stood at the bottom of the stairs but
didn't speak. He sat down at the table and picked up a comic. He
couldn't read it. His mother spoke.

'Do you want to go on a message for me?'

John feigned interest in his comic.

'Where to?'

'Warwick Street, Annie Hood's.'

'What for?'

'To pass on some books.'

'When? Now?'

'Yes, now.'

Annie Hood was old and not very good on her feet; she
lived in the basement of a large terraced house on the corner of

65

Mill Street and Warwick Street. His mother would visit and go to the shops for her; she would also give her books. The books were usually about saints and martyrs, but some were women's fiction.

As he walked up Warwick Street with the parcel of books John thought of ways to persuade his mother to let him go to see The Beatles. Going to Annie Hood's wouldn't do any harm. John arrived, went down the stone steps to Annie's and knocked. It took a while for her to open the door. It was always the same. She was almost deaf and she needed a walking stick.

The door eventually opened.

'Hello John! Hello! Come in! Come in!' Annie half-screamed.

The room was in semi-darkness. The walls of her living room were painted green. Even though Annie's lights were on, the room was still dull: Annie had gaslights and that didn't help. John guessed that the Corporation was going to pull the house down so the landlord wasn't too bothered with electric lights. A large iron grate sat in the chimney breast surrounding an oven. The oven door had a long brass handle with wide hinges. A tall mantelpiece stood over the oven along with an iron rod running the length of the chimney breast with some of Annie's washing draped over it. John knew that one of her neighbours would come down and light the gaslights for her but Annie was able to turn them off herself, by pulling a chain on the lamp. John supposed it wouldn't be long before the Corporation made Annie's home a bomdie. Lately John had noticed increasing numbers of bomdies around his neighbourhood.

Annie's eyes focused on the brown paper parcel. He passed the bundle to her. She leaned her walking stick against a chair, placed the books on the table and took the string off. When the books were revealed, her eyes lit up.

'Oh I haven't read that, or that. And I haven't read that one for ages, I'll read that again.'

John smiled. Annie was happy. She told him to sit down and asked him if he wanted a cup of tea.

'No, thanks.'

'Some toast?'

'No thanks.'

'A tea cake?'

'No thanks, Mrs. Hood.

'An apple?'

'Not hungry thanks.'

John wanted to go but Annie talked on and on and John thought that maybe that's what happened when you became old: you got boring.

'Can I have a glass of water please, Mrs. Hood?'

'Yes certainly, son.'

When Annie came back with the water she said, 'Just you at home without a job, eh? Are you being a good boy, helping your mam around the house?'

John held the glass of water to his mouth. *The wallpapering.* He put the glass down without drinking.

'I've got to go now Mrs. Hood, see ya,' he said suddenly. He didn't wait for her to open the door. He let himself out and ran across the road. He didn't even think about looking out for traffic and as soon as he got home he set about helping his mother until all walls were stripped.

There were lots of cracks in the plaster and some of it had come away from the wall where he'd been scraping off the wallpaper, but he wasn't bothered. He'd helped his mother and not only that, he'd stripped over half of the room himself, even though he'd started much later than his mother.

His mother stood at the bottom of the stairs and looked around the room, 'It looks better already,' she said and smiled at John.

'I'll brush up the rest of the small scraps and that's it; we've done a good job, haven't we mam?' John smiled back at his mam and then he said, 'I've made a pot of tea. Sit down, mam, you must be tired.'

He smiled again and pulled out a chair from the table for his mother.

'Shall I give the skirting boards a wipe over with a damp cloth, like you said, while we're waiting for the tea to draw?'

'Alright John, alright,' said his mother. 'You can go.'

'Yis!'

'But I want to speak to Steve Costello and Kevin and Keith Dunleavy before you go.'

'Yeah mam, I'll bring them here, I will, I will.'

He took a couple of library books and went up to his bedroom to wait until it was time to call for Mike. The books were on ancient Greece and Rome. John would tell his uncle about Alexander the Great and his famous battles and how he travelled as far as India; that he was only young when he died. John had told his uncle that Alexander ate something poisonous that killed him. A meat pie from Elsie's, suggested his uncle.

Many a time he tried to get Mike to go with him but Mike wasn't interested so he went on his own. He told Tommy Sanderson about a new library book he'd taken out on ancient Greek history. Tommy was older than John and didn't live in the street. John would hang around with him now and again and swap comics. Tommy told him a joke; John didn't know it was a joke at first but thought it was a puzzle.

'What was purple and conquered half the world?' asked Tommy.

'I don't know,' replied John.

'Alexander the Grape.'

He didn't understand it until Tommy explained it to him. John guessed they're the kind of jokes they tell in secondary school. He put the book down and went back downstairs. His mother stood at the sink washing clothes.

'Has Mike Costello called, mam?'

'No. Go to Elsie's and get me some potatoes.' She noticed the library book John held, 'Why don't you call for Tommy Sanderson on the way back from Elsie's?'

'Er, yeah I will.'

Go to Elsie's then call for Tommy Sanderson. He didn't think so. He knew his mother would like him to go to see The Beatles with Tommy Sanderson, because she thought Tommy would look out for him but John knew he could look after himself. A couple of months before John and Tommy threw pieces of broken roof slates at a tin can. John held the slate too tight and when he threw it his finger cut open. He didn't feel anything at first but half an inch of his finger had opened out along the tip where he pressed onto the edge of the slate. He looked dumbly at the cut and the blood that poured out then shook his hand, like the boys in school would do after they'd been given the cane. He didn't notice that when he shook his finger he rained blood all over Tommy. Tommy looked in amusement at John, not noticing the blood being sprayed towards him. Tommy was covered in spots of blood, on his shirt, his trousers and on his face. Then Tommy noticed the splats of blood on his shirt then touched his face. He looked in shock at the blood on his hands and immediately began to cry, then scream and ran off. John watched Tommy run away and didn't know whether to laugh or feel sorry for him. He could have told his mother about that when she suggested going to see The Beatles with Tommy. When he was lost in Calderstones Park he knew he was only a kid but Tommy was thirteen. John thought that, mam's think they know loads of things and they do, but there are loads of things they don't know.

As he walked along the back of the street to Elsie's, Mike's next-door neighbour, Mrs. Williams, washed her backyard.

'Where are you off to John?'

'On a message for my mam.'

'Where's that?'

'Just up the road, see ya.'

Mrs. Williams was alright but she was a bit nosy. She had no kids, so John didn't know if that had something to do with it. But she always wanted to know what people were doing or where you were going and she'd chase the kids away from her front door if they were noisy. The lamp post used as a swing stood outside hers and Mike's house. If a swing was made on the lamp post and the kids were too noisy she'd chase them. A month ago Mike's mother sat on her front door step and watched the kids play football. Mrs. Williams came out to move the kids off.

'Go on clear off you're making too much noise.'

'They're only playing Phyllis,' said Mike's mother.

Mrs. William didn't notice her sitting on the step she looked down then looked away.

'I know they're only playing Betty but they're noisy.'

Mrs. Williams disappeared back inside. His own mother told him, 'you never hear your own kids'.

*   *   *

John came out of Elsie's with the bag of potatoes. A man passed him walking towards the docks; he carried a large packed duffle bag over his shoulder. John knew the man was going to his ship. He was sure it was easy to go away to sea. Marty Jones had told him. Marty had gone away to sea at sixteen. When he arrived home from a trip he'd be in a taxi. Sometimes he was tanned. The kids would all want to carry his duffle bag the couple of yards from the taxi to Marty's house. And Marty never failed to give the kids money if they asked him if he had any coppers he didn't want.

When Marty first started to go away to sea, John found out when he was shipping out and followed him. He didn't remember how he knew; he guessed he must have heard his mother and Marty's mother talking. John followed him for few minutes, down to the Dock Road. Marty kept on chasing him home. John would hide and then follow him again. He hid behind a truck that was loaded with sacks of coffee. When he'd peeked out from behind the back wheel he couldn't see Marty. He ran and looked but he'd lost him. And now the smell of coffee reminded him of the time he hid behind a flat bed truck stacked with Brazilian beans while he tried to catch sight of Marty Jones.

When he arrived home his mother was reading a paper.

'Has Mike Costello called, mam?'

'No, maybe it's a bit early for him, lad.'

'Did you call for Tommy Sanderson?'

'Yeah, he wasn't in.'

John told himself to remember that one for confession.

'Do all the other lads' mams know they're going to see The Beatles?'

'Yeah.'

John wondered if that was a lie too; he wasn't sure. But he told himself to remember that one as well for confession too, just in case.

He picked up a comic and watched his mother reading her paper. He had looked at the *News of the World* a couple of times; Mike Costello's dad bought it. Mike had said there were some dirty stories in it, about a woman who worked as a model. John had sneaked it up to his bedroom and read it. The story said that the model had a thirty-six inch bust but John couldn't believe it. He found a twelve-inch ruler and measured down from the top of his chest three times. It went right down past his knees. He read the story again. He thought they must have got the measurements wrong. He thought about asking Mike about it, but he didn't want Mike to know he didn't know.

He looked up from his comic. He said, 'Mam are we moving?'

'What do you mean?'

'I mean going to live on the outskirts.'

'Why do you say that, son?'

'Nothing. It's just that people are moving out, aren't they? The Corporation's knocking loads of houses down.'

'Yes, but that doesn't mean we have to move out. We can stay around here; the Corporation could offer us a house nearby.

Why, would you like to move to the outskirts, with lots of new houses and fields for your football?'

'Nar, the buses on the outskirts are last.' His mother looked at him. John had forgotten she didn't know.

'The thing is, John, where we are now is handy for your dad and Peter's job and Mary's; and all our friends and family are around here. I want to stay around here. If anything I'd like to move up, nearer to the Church.'

'So we won't be moving out to the outskirts then?'

'I wouldn't think so, not if we can help it.'

'What about the barracks? Wouldn't my dad want to move to be near that?'

'Well, we're not that far from Aigburth Road now; as a matter of fact moving to the outskirts would make the barracks awkward to get to.'

It made sense what his mother said about the barracks. A few months before he'd heard his mother and Uncle Jim arguing.

'That's why Cleary goes the barracks, Kathleen to get away from you and your preaching. He hardly gets a break from you and your Church.'

Uncle Jim would call his brother-in-law Cleary when John's dad wasn't there. John didn't think Uncle Jim was being mean when he called his dad by his surname; sometimes his mother did as well.

His mother would reply, 'You don't know you, Jim Mulhearn, you're ignorant. You think you know the lot. You'd do well to go to Church yourself. Then maybe you'd spend more time at home with your wife instead of with your mates in the pub, poor woman.' She'd say 'I've said my piece' and turn away.

When she stopped talking, Uncle Jim became angry and when she talked about the Church or the pub or Auntie Sheila he only got more frustrated and angrier. The only way Uncle Jim could try to get his mother angry was by criticizing the Church.

'Father O'Rourke, he's always in Saint Pat's Club', he'd say. 'Where does he get the money from? I'll tell you where; the money off the plate on a Sunday. That's his money for a bevvy, gets polluted on your money. Great, isn't it?'

John's mother would reply, 'You'll go to hell you, James Mulhearn, you will. God's listening; he can hear every word you say. I'll pray for you.'

Uncle Jim would shake his head and say things under his breath. There was one time though, when John's mother lost her temper with her brother. It was six months ago.

It was mid week, five o'clock when Uncle Jim had finished work early and been to the pub. He had called into John's house. John's mother had told her brother he was welcome to stay for his tea. Peter and John's dad weren't home. She prepared the tea while Uncle Jim talked to John about football and to Mary about boyfriends. Later Uncle Jim asked about John's dad.

'He's not back from work yet and when he comes in he's getting a quick wash an' shave and going to the barracks,' said John's mother. That was it.

'Ya know what, Kath? You're driving Cleary from his own house with your preaching.'

'You're talking daft.'

'That's why he goes the barracks ya know, to get away from all the talk about the Church,' said Uncle Jim.'

'You don't know what you're talking about.'

'Don't I? Cleary gets in and out from work and up to the barracks, otherwise he'd have priests and the Church battering his ears.'

'You should go to Church; wouldn't do you no harm. Go to confession before you go, as well,' said his mother.

'Go to confession! Church!'

'Yes, it would do you good if you went to Church.'

'Church! Hey listen Kath, don't tell me about the Church. What about the new priest, Father Hanlon, and the new young housekeeper. Hey, what about that?' He smiled like he'd caught his sister out. He looked chuffed with himself. 'Yeah some housekeeper she is; we could all do with a housekeeper like that. Yeah, smashing that. Holy orders; I'll order some of that.'

No one spoke for a while. John looked at Mary; he didn't know what was going on. Mary looked at him with a straight face and put a finger across her lips. Suddenly John's mother without a word stood up and grabbed the yard brush from near the sink.

'That's enough! That's enough,' she shouted, 'Get out! Get out!' She pulled open the kitchen door and began to brush Uncle Jim out into the backyard. He didn't know what was going on; John didn't know either. John wasn't too sure if even Mary knew. It looked mad. Uncle Jim spluttered some words as he grabbed his coat off the back of the chair. He tried not to notice as the head of the yard brush banged against his ankles while he put his coat on. He tried not to look too bothered, as if it happened all the time. He attempted to speak as he put his coat on but couldn't be heard as John's mother shouted.

'Out! Out! Out! You're not staying in this house with talk like that!'

And when he was brushed into the backyard his sister slammed the door shut, then locked it. John thought, 'This is great; this is smashing, just like the Charlie Chaplin films. They should have stuff like this on the telly.' John turned to Mary to speak but she gave him a look and shook her head. John thought it was funny but at the same time he felt sorry for his uncle. Uncle Jim was a big man and he had been brushed out of the house into the backyard and it was pitch black out there. It was in the middle of the winter and the backyard door had two bolts on it, at the top and bottom. John didn't think Uncle Jim would be able to see them in the dark, especially after his mother closed the curtains. She switched off the television, sat down and lit a Woodbine, her hand shaking. It was quiet. John waited to hear the bolts being dragged back on the backyard door, but nothing. They waited, then his mother opened the curtains and shouted.

'You'd better get going, Jim Mulhearn, or I'll be out there with a bucket of water, even if you are in the lavatory.'

John felt sorry for Uncle Jim that night, One minute he was talking to him about centre forwards and to Mary about new boy friends, waiting to have his tea and rubbing his hands; the next thing he was nearly walking home with a yard brush up his bum.

*   *   *

John stopped outside Mike's open front door. He waited impatiently, and when Mike appeared he said, 'Are you going?'

'Yeah, what about you? You're still going, aren't you? You said you were. Your mam hasn't said you can't go, has she?'

'No, I've just got to let her know who I'm going with, that's all. Is your Steve still going?'

'Yeah, but he's going with some lads from their class.'

'Oh!'

'What's up?'

'Nothing, let's call for Kevin and Keith.'

The Dunleavys' house was at the end of the street. It was different to the other houses; it was the only house that was detached. It was also larger than the other houses and separated by an entry. The entry had a small arch twelve-foot above the entrance that connected the Dunleavys to their next-door neighbour's, Mrs. Simpson's. Some of the older kids would climb up onto the arch by pressing their feet and hands on the sides of the entry walls. A few weeks earlier Steve had sat on top of the arch and spat down at some little kids. Mrs. Simpson had come out and seen him.

'You dirty little sod, spitting, I'm going to get a bucket of water for you,' she shouted

John and Mike kicked a ball and stopped to watch. Steve pushed his feet and arms against the gable end walls and climbed down crab-like as quickly as he could. He jumped the last three feet, slipped and tore his trousers. He stood up and looked at the rip in his trousers, then ran down the entry to the back of the houses.

One of the little kids shouted after him, 'Come back! Come back and fight me, ya friggin' coward.'

Everyone laughed, but the little kids ran off when Mrs. Simpson came out with a bucket.

John and Mike stopped outside Keith and Kevin's door.

'Now Kevin, now Keith!' Mike sang through the letter box.

Mike took a step back and looked up at the Dunleavy's house. 'There's no one in,' he said.

'Where've they gone?'

'Oh bleedin' hell. I know, they told me last night, I forgot,' said Mike. 'They were going to town with their mam to get new shoes and they had to go the Eye Hospital.'

'What? Why didn't you tell me?'

'Forgot.'

'Flippin' 'eck, they could be ages in the Eye Hospital. And my mam won't let me go if it's only us two.'

'She won't? Bleedin' 'ell!'

'What are we going to do?'

'*We*, I don't know what you're going to do but I'm going,' said Mike.

There was a long pause.

'Can you think of anyone else?' said John.

'No, they'll all be going in their own gangs, won't they? I know! What about Maureen Coleman?'

'No!' said John, hoping his face hadn't gone red. 'Bloody hell,' he thought. 'Maureen.'

'Why not?' said Mike, sensing he was on to something. 'She's from the street, she plays with us now and again, and she's the same age, so she's not a kid.'

'No Mike,' said John. 'We can't go with a girl. There'll be loads of girls up there to see The Beatles but we'd look soft going with a girl, especially if someone from your school or my school saw us. It's a long way to Princes Road; someone would definitely see us.'

John still felt embarrassed when he thought about Maureen. A few months before, the Coleman's television had broken and John asked his mother could Maureen come and watch theirs. He liked her. And that week, the more she came round the more he'd liked her. It wasn't the same as the way he liked his mates; it was different. And they didn't just watch television. They'd looked at his comics and library books, played hang-the-man, ludo and snakes and ladders in the parlour. And even though she only lived a few doors away, his mother made John walk Maureen home and wait until her mother opened the door.

On the night Maureen told him that they were having a new television delivered, they'd talked as they'd walked back to Maureen's and when they got there she'd turned round and kissed him. At first John hardly knew what was going on, but then he'd kissed her back. He'd just done it; he hadn't thought. It was only a few seconds, then Maureen had turned away as the door opened and she said good night as the door closed.

John had stood there in the dark, like a lost soul. He'd felt daft and good at the same time; he'd never felt like that before. He didn't tell anyone because if the gang found out they'd definitely boot him out, he knew that much. But the gang never did find out. And now Mike was suggesting Maureen come with them. But what if she got all excited the way girls did when they saw The Beatles? She might get that excited she'd start trying to kiss the gob off him.

'No Mike,' said John, trying to make his voice sound like its usual self. 'We can't call for Maureen. We don't want a girl coming with us.'

'So who do you reckon we could call for then?'

'Er, I don't know.'

'Well I can't think of anyone.'

'I know. Let's give Billy Mogan a call.'

'Billy Mogan?'

'Yeah, you know him, his mam's dead. He goes to Saint Pat's. But he doesn't really know anyone round here so if he's going he'll be on his own.'

'Dead smart that, good thinking, John,' said Mike. 'Billy's coloured isn't he?'

'He was the last time I saw him. So what?'

'Well we're going up Prinny Road and there are loads of coloured lads up there and Billy will know them because that's where he's from.'

John didn't want Billy to go with them for that reason and what Mike said made him feel like a cheat.

'He's a mate, Mike,' said John. 'Let's go down to see if he wants to go with us, then after dinner get off. Do you know what time The Beatles are getting in the airport for?'

'Er, I think the, er, plane leaves London at two o'clock and lands at Speke Airport at half two. So they'll be going along Prinny Road at three o'clock.'

'What? That doesn't sound right.'

'It is! It is! Because they're going in a jet and they can go a thousand miles an hour.'

'Maybe they do but they've got to go to Speke Airport, then to the Town Hall, they're not bleeding landing in Prinny Road. It'll take longer than that.'

'But them jets are fast, you know.'

He told himself he should have known better than to ask Mike. Mike was his best mate, but John was glad he wasn't in Saint Patrick's; he was sure he'd make a show of him.

'Look Mike, I'll go in and find out the time The Beatles are coming and give you a knock in about ten minutes, alright? We don't wanna go to Billy's and not know what time to be there, do we?'

'Yeah, alright, ten minutes; see you later.'

*   *   *

He sat in the parlour and read the local paper. He knew he should have looked at it last night. He'd felt like telling Mike to piss off before. He wondered if his mother and the priest were right about swearing being a sin, even when you were only thinking it. After all, he told himself, 'no one can hear you.'

'God can hear you.' That's what Monsignor Curry would say.

Maybe he was right John thought, because when he went to confession the priest always asked, 'Have you had any impure thoughts?' Was thinking of swearing words, impure thoughts? John didn't know. He guessed impure thoughts were thinking about nude women and shaggin'. But what was shaggin'? John didn't know. He knew it was to do with what a man and woman do in bed and it had to do with your willy. None of the others in the gang knew but they said they knew. He wondered if what he was thinking now was impure thoughts. If it was, he wasn't going to tell the priest. Nar, couldn't tell the priest that.

He turned a page:

In Melbourne, 42,000 people paid in advance for their six performances. In Brisbane, 20,000 paying customers in two nights. Sydney, another record - 22,000 at two shows, after their successful tour of the Far East and Australia.

'No a bit further on there.'

They will depart from Heathrow airport at 3.30pm and arrive at Speke airport at approximately 4.15pm. Tens of thousands of excited teenagers are expected to line the route from the airport to the Town Hall. All police leave in the local area has been cancelled.

He estimated The Beatles would be at Princes Road around half past four; lots of time. Mike and his jet - daft get, he wants a jet up his soddin' bum; that would wake him up.

Twenty minutes later Mike called.

'I thought you were going to give me a knock?'

'I was, but I had to read the paper, didn't I, and work out the times. It's going to be ages yet; well after dinner.'

'Are you sure? I mean them jets, they're fast.'

'Sod the jets, Mike, I'm telling you. Do you want me to go in and get the paper? You can read it yourself, you know.'

'No, no it's alright, I believe you. So you're sure then?'

'I'm sure. The paper said they're going to the Town Hall about five o'clock. Then they're going to get something to eat, with the Lord Mayor. And then they're going to the Odeon in London Road, to see that picture they made. If you don't believe me I'll go in and get the paper. It's only in the parlour, I'll get it.'

'No! No, it's just - you know, we don't wanna miss them. What shall we do now, go to Billy Mogan's?'

'Yeah, call for Billy.' He turned around. 'Mam! I'm going out - be back after.'

'Well don't go straight there - I want to see all of you before you go. Careful of the roads; bless yourself.'

Mike looked to see if he was going to bless himself from the plastic holy water fount nailed to the inside of the door frame, but John never. He was able to bless himself without Mike knowing, with his tongue, on the roof of his mouth, then the bottom; left then right, the way his mother had told him, but he didn't even do that. He just wanted to go. He knew Mike believed his mother was too religious but Mike hardly mentioned it; sometimes they made a joke about it, but not often.

'There's going to be loads of people up there, you know?' said Mike, 'The telly men with cameras will be there, our Steve reckons. And there'll be fellas up there taking pictures for the papers and magazines. You know who the ones are that get their picture in the paper? They're the ones that stand out, that look different; that's how they get in the paper.'

'Like the way the girls have pictures of The Beatles pinned to their jumpers or have The Beatles names knitted in scarves?'

'That's it! That's it! That's what I mean! You see them; they're the ones you see on the telly. I've got a jumper. I think I might wear it, might get my picture in the paper.'

'It hasn't got their names on it, has it?'

'Nar, don't be soft; it's only a jumper.' Mike kicked a stone. 'It's nothing really; I was just thinking about it.' Mike suddenly looked embarrassed as they walked down the slope at the back of their street to Beaufort Street. The boys stopped at the bottom of the slope. Mike looked around.

'Look out for Albie McInerney,'

'Why? What have you done?'

'Nothing!'

'Have you been calling him?'

'No! No! I haven't.'

Mike shook his head, but John knew he was lying. John knew that if Albie saw them they would be chased, and it didn't matter who he caught; they would be the ones who were given a belt or a kick. The kids would call Albie "Scobie Bressley" after the jockey, for a chase. That was the name of Albie's favourite jockey. Or they'd call him "three names".

'Come on, three names, give us a chase! Three names! Three names! Come on, soft lad.' Three names: Albie, Mac and Ernie.

'Albie won't get us,' said Mike. 'You look over there,' Mike nodded to his right, 'and I'll look over here,' and he did the same to his left.

'You should have told us.'

'Doesn't matter, does it? Anyway he's touched, he doesn't mind. I know, if he comes from your side we'll say like the cartoon on the telly, what's it called? *Snaggle Puss*, "exit, stage right," and if he comes from this side we'll say: "exit, stage left". Good that, isn't it?'

'Yeah, but what happens if he comes from behind? Do you say, "exit, up your bum"?' Mike laughed. John thought he would, 'Come on, let's run.'

They slowed down as they turned into Hill Street.

'Do you think Billy Mogan will want to go with us then, John?'

'Don't know. Yeah, I think so. Everyone's going, aren't they? Even Albie?'

As soon as he'd said it he felt bad.

'Oh yeah, think he will. Yeah, bet he'll have a Beatle wig on; that'd be a laugh.'

John felt worse. He told himself to learn to keep his mouth shut. 'Come on let's hurry up.' John ran again.

Billy lived on the fourth and top landing of a tenement block that gave a view into the docks and the Pier Head. After they had climbed to the first landing they looked over.

'What are you going to do if Billy isn't in, or isn't going?' asked Mike.

'I don't know. What are you going to do?'

Mike shrugged and went up to the next landing, John followed. On the next floor the boys leaned over the landing again. On the opposite side, on the corner with Grafton Street, stood the Southern Hospital.

'When you get to Billy's landing you can see right in; see the beds and nurses,' said John.

'I know.'

John wasn't too sure if Mike did know. Thinking about it, he wasn't even too sure if Mike had been to Billy's before.

'You can see right down to the Pier Head from the top, you know?' said John.

'I know.'

'And from Billy's bedroom you can see the ships getting launched from the shipyards in Cammell Laird's. We seen one a while back. It was great. You were with us, weren't you?'

'Yeah that's right, I was.'

John had been in Billy's bedroom lots of times and he knew you couldn't see Cammell Laird's from it. Caryl Gardens across the road blocked the view of the shipyard.

'Look at that,' said Mike pointing to words chalked on the landing wall: '"Billy Mo shits on the po".'

'Let's try and get it off,' said John, and he rubbed at the chalk.

'Why?'

'Because it's not nice, that's why.'

'Not nice - you're soft you.'

'Come on. You wouldn't like it if it was about you. You wouldn't like it if your mam or someone in your house seen it.'

'But his mam's dead, isn't she?'

'That's not the point. Come on.'

The boys rubbed at the chalk, then spat at it and scrubbed it with the soles of their shoes. Then, when the words were hardly visible, they walked on up the stairs.

'I've hardly got any spit left,' said Mike.

John ignored him. 'You can see all kinds from up here,' he said, as they arrived at the top landing.

'I'm knackered,' said Mike.

'You shouldn't smoke, then.'

'I don't! I don't! Honest! Just a few drags from our Steve, that's all. Don't tell your mam, ya know, because she might tell mine and she'll batter me and so will our Steve.'

'I won't, I won't,' said John. 'Don't worry.' But he'd only been joking about Mike smoking. He hadn't known he sometimes had a few drags from their Steve.

'Trust Billy to live on the top, eh?' said John.

'Yeah, trust Billy,' said Mike. 'It's smart up here though, isn't it?'

'I told you it was, but you've been up here before so you know that, don't ya?' John looked at him.

'Yeah, yeah I've been here before. I was just saying it's smart.' He looked over the landing.

Billy's house was the last one along the landing. John pushed open the letterbox.

'Now Billee!' he shouted.

'How long has his mam been dead?'

'Bleedin' hell, shut up!'

'I'm only asking. You don't have to throw a wobbler.'

John shook his head. Mike shouldn't be let out on his own, he thought, he really shouldn't.

Mike leaned over the landing and played with the pole on the washing line. The door opened a couple of inches and Billy's six-year-old brother, Christopher, looked out.

'Hiya. Is your Billy in?' asked John.

Billy's brother looked at them, then turned away. Mike shrugged and leaned over the landing again.

Billy came to the door.

'Alright, John, what you doing?'

Mike didn't turn round.

'We were gonna go up to Prinny Road after dinner, to see The Beatles. Do you wanna come?'

'What time?'

'We'll get off around two o'clock or half past,'
Mike still leaned over the landing.

'Half two or that eh Mike?' John gave Mike a small kick as he spoke.

'Yeah, that's alright, come with us if you want.' Mike spoke without enthusiasm.

'That's good of ya,' said Billy to Mike without meaning it, 'but the thing is I've got to look after our Christopher, so…'

'I thought you had sisters?' said Mike

'I have, but they're all at bleeding work, aren't they?'

'Alright, alright, keep your hair on; I was only asking.'

'What I was gonna say was, I could take him to my Auntie Beth's by your house,' said Billy. His auntie lived in the next block to Geoffrey Budd's.

'Okay,' said John.

'I'd let you come in but Christopher might tell our Sheila.'

'It's alright.'

John knew if he'd been on his own, Billy would have brought him in.

'Do you know any good places to watch from?' said John.

'Yeah,' said Mike. 'Do you? Do you know any good specs?'

'I think so. Yeah, wait there. I might know a good one.'

84

'Great,' said Mike 'because the cameras will be up there for the telly and the men with the cameras for the papers. We might get our pictures taken or be on the telly; if we have a good spec the men from the telly might see us.'

'If you get me five bob, I'll guarantee a great spec,' said Billy. 'You'll see everything and the telly cameras will see you as well. You'll be standing right up over everyone and everyone will see you; you'll get a great look at The Beatles.'

Five bob. John looked at Billy.

'See you later,' said John.

Now Billy was coming John didn't need the twins - *but five bob.*

They were halfway along the landing when Billy shouted, 'Hey John, it'll be fab. Fabtastic!' and he gave a thumbs-up. 'Fabtastic! See yas later.' He put his hand up with his fingers stretched wide and mouthed "five bob" and laughed.

John and Mike went down the stairs. Mike was quiet.

'What's up?' asked John.

'Him! He's bleedin' daft; soft in the bloody head, laughing and telling us we need five bob.'

'It's a lot of money but it would be worth it though, wouldn't it?'

'I haven't got five bob, and if I had, I bloody well wouldn't give it to him. And what about fabtastic? I thought it was fab. It's fab, isn't it?'

'I don't know. Maybe he's right, maybe that's what fab's short for. Fabtastic. You know, an abbreviation.'

'What?'

'You know, like when you shorten something.'

'Like what?'

'Er ... er'

'Yeah? Go on.'

'Alright, like, er… Johnny - that's short for John.'

'How can it be? Johnny makes it bleedin' longer.'

'No! No! I didn't mean that, no. What I meant was, er, like Pat. There y'are. Pat. That's short for Patrick, Saint Pat's, and Mike's short for Michael and, er, Bill's short for Billy and...' but John couldn't think of anything else.

'But they're just lads' names,' said Mike. 'What about other words shortened? Tell me some other words, clever Dick.'

John couldn't think. That's the problem when you try to sound clever, he thought, sometimes you're not. He stopped in the stairwell to think, but Mike didn't wait. He thought he had John.

'I know!' John shouted after Mike. 'I know. Airie.'

'What?'

'Airie, deaf lugs. Airie for aeroplane, and here's another: copper for policeman and Seffie Park for Sefton Park and - here y'are, what about this one? Prinny Road for Princes Road.'

'Alright, alright! Big head!'

They came out the block. Mike never spoke.

'Here y'are Mike, where are we now? Think of it; see if you can get that one.'

'You trying to be funny?'

'No I'm not; think about it.'

'Hilly... oh yeah, Hill Street. So Hilly's short for Hill Street, I've got it.'

'You've got it; that's good, you soft get,' John said to himself. John knew he shouldn't call him, but Mike could be hard work sometimes.

'Shall we go back the way we came or walk up and go the long way round to miss Albie?' said Mike.

'Go back the same way, I think. Albie's gone in for his dinner now.'

'So we'll walk back along Beauie - Beaufort Street – eh, abbreviated. Look at this John! Look at this!'

John thought Mike was going to wet himself.

Mike pointed up at the pub's name, 'The Neppy; the Neptune. Abbreviated.'

'I've got another one,' said Mike.

John looked at him. Oh soddin' hell, I'm going to have this all bleedin' day now. What have I started?

Chapter Seven
WANTING

Glasgow was a skilled worker's city without ghettos: Its
workingmen and women at large rejected sectarianism
and embraced socialism. In Liverpool this never happened
before the Second- World War. In Glasgow it was possible to
believe in the gradual development of socialism as working- men
left Liberalism behind and moved to Labour, and some to
revolutionary socialism; in Liverpool the only hope was
industrial riot in which the dominant organisations of the city
were temporary put to one side. Glasgow workingmen were
good socialists but lousy rioters; Liverpool workingmen
were quite the reverse.

J, Smith, *Labour Tradition in Glasgow and Liverpool*

As John went through his front door, he heard his dad and Uncle
Jim in the back room.

'Can't you have a word, Tom?' said Uncle Jim. 'She's your
soddin' wife.'

'Can't you have a word, Jim?' John's dad replied. 'She's
your bleedin' sister.'

John went into the kitchen. His dad and Uncle Jim were
wallpapering. Some of the wallpaper they had put up had been
ripped and patched in places. Some of it was already peeling from
the corners. Scraps of pasted wallpaper and wallpaper that had torn
in two lay on the floor. His dad and Uncle Jim had their backs to
John. His uncle stood on a chair holding a strip of wallpaper while
his dad brushed it onto the wall.

'Hold it straight, Jim!'

'I'm no good at this lark, Tom; shouldn't the landlord do all this?'

'Ask Kath.'

'Have you got any money for a pint?' Uncle Jim looked as if he'd rather be pushing drawing pins into his forehead than wallpapering. He turned and noticed John in the doorway and smiled.

'Here's the man himself. Now we can have a break. Kath! Your lad's home!'

John went to the backyard where his mother was taking sheets off the washing line. He was about to mention going to see The Beatles with Billy Mogan when she put some pegs into her mouth. He decided he'd wait until after dinner. His dad and Uncle Jim tidied up the scraps of wallpaper.

'But the thing is, Tom, we're never gonna get anywhere without them officially recognizing us; that's why we've got to keep pushing. You never get anything without trying, and a bit of hardship's just part and parcel of the game.'

'I know, Jim, I know that. I've been down there long enough to understand what you're saying but we're not putting bread on the table doing this, are we?' His dad turned around. 'Alright son? Not going up there?' He pretended to play a guitar.

'I'm going up there after my dinner.'

'Better wash your hands.'

John went to the sink.

'Tom,' continued Uncle Jim, 'it doesn't matter about putting bread on the table. Everyone's skint once in a while. Look, I'm not pulling rank on you but I've been around; I've been skint more times than I've been flush. I mean the likes of us, we're always gonna be a bit skint now and then. But what we're talking about here is more important than that. Let's face it, Tom, the Union's in bed with the ship-owners and the Labour Board. It's bad enough fighting the bosses, but when you're fighting your own or what's supposed to be your soddin' own... years ago when I first went away to sea I was only a kid and I always remember what this old stoker said. We were talking about work - politics and stuff like that. And I said something like, "Yeah, life's hard". Then, know what he said? "No. Life's not hard. It's just other bastards making it hard". And that's true. What you need is dignity in the work process... just dignity in the work process.'

'I'm not arguing with you,' said John's dad. 'I know what you're saying. But sometimes we can go too far.'

'Oh, for fuck's sake Tom! How can we go too far by sticking together?'

'Jim! Jim!' said John's dad, and out of the corner of his eye John could see his dad jerk his head in his direction. 'I'll tell you what, lad,' his dad said, 'your hands must be rotten, bleedin' minty, the time you're taking there.'

John turned round.

'Have you been working down a coal mine?' said his dad, and he winked at Uncle Jim.

John knew what his dad was on about; he didn't like John ear-wigging. But it was always the same when Uncle Jim came round, John would listen as Uncle Jim and his father or his mother argued.

'Nearly done,' said John, smiling. 'What's the hurry?'

'Don't you be cheeky, now,' said his dad. 'Go and ask your mam what's for dinner.'

'Just drying my hands first,' said John as he picked up the tea towel and went out the back door. He repeated his dad's question to his mother in the backyard.

'What?' said his mam, 'When am I going to do his dinner?'

'Yeah.'

'And when am I going to do Uncle Jim's dinner as well?'

'Yeah.'

'Haven't they got a pair of hands?' John's mother looked through the kitchen window. 'Sitting on their... it doesn't matter lad,' she said, turning back to John. 'I'll see to them.' She collected the rest of the sheets off the line and took them inside. John followed.

His dad and his Uncle Jim sat at the table.

His mother put the washing basket next to the sink.

'Hello lads,' said his mother. 'I've just been told you're hungry. You must have got an appetite arguing with the fellas down the docks. Would you like me to do you a nice roast dinner? I'll even cut the meat up into small pieces for you, like you do for the babies.'

'What are you going on about, Kathleen? It's not Sunday,' his dad said.

'I know it's not Sunday, and you're not babies. What are you sending the lad out to me for? Can't you do your own dinner? Or are you too tired after your hard half-day's work?'

'Ah, don't be like that Kathleen,' said Uncle Jim.

His mother didn't look at her brother; she looked at John's dad.

'Haven't you looked in the larder?' she said.

'There's nothing there, girl, I've looked.' John's mother still didn't look at her brother.

'There's eggs,' said his mother.

'I don't fancy them.'

John's mother nearly looked at her brother but stopped herself. 'And there's cheese.'

'Don't like cheese, you know that,' said Uncle Jim.

This time John's mother did look at her brother. She stared at him. But she spoke to John's dad. 'But you eat cheese, Cleary. You like eggs. What's stopping you?'

'Oh hey Kathleen; don't start. I can't be eating while your Jim's got nothing to eat, can I?'

'Oh I see. You do the same work, drink the same beer but can't eat the same food. That makes sense.'

She turned to her brother. 'I'll tell you what, Jim Mulhearn, you'd eat what's in the larder if you were hungry, wouldn't you? So you can't be hungry. That's your problem, Jim Mulhearn; our mam spoilt you. You couldn't do nothing wrong with my mam. You were always her favourite; you wanted for nothing off my mam, nothing. Big man? Mammy's lad, that's what you are. You've sailed the seven seas and you can't even eat a bit of cheese.'

'Kathleen, you know I've never eaten cheese and I don't fancy eggs. Can't you send the lad down to the shops for a couple of ounces of boiled ham?'

'Boiled ham! Boiled ham! It's Friday, ya heathen.'

John's dad put his hand to his forehead as if he were keeping the sun out of his eyes. Uncle Jim rubbed his chin.

'Oh yeah, forgot about that Kathleen, er, forgot about that. Again.'

But all his mother did was pick up her purse from the top of the television and open it. She gazed out of the window into the backyard. 'I haven't got any housekeeping left,' she said. 'What's the lad to go to the shop with, a smile and a promise?'

'Oh yeah, sorry, yeah, I wasn't thinking. Here y'are, son. Here's some money.' John's dad stood up quickly and dug into his pocket. 'And keep thre'pence for going.'

'Thanks dad!'

'Get a pot of salmon paste and a pot of crab paste son,' his mother said. 'And your lace is undone.' She turned to her brother.

'Salmon alright? Crab alright? Won't upset your stomach will it, Jim? I know how delicate your poor old stomach can be.'

John's mother took some sheets out of the washing basket and placed them over a chair. Uncle Jim never said anything; he just looked at John's dad as he shook his head.

John's mother turned back to the men. 'And don't think you're just going to sit there while the lad runs around after you. Make yourself useful; do some bread.'

His dad went to the larder and cut a loaf; Uncle Jim followed him and picked up the butter.

'Your lace John - tie it before you go to Elsie's,' said his mother. 'How many times do I have to tell you?' His mother put some wet clothes from the sink into the basket and went out into the backyard.

'Alright, mam.' John put the money in his pocket, then lifted his foot up onto the chair to tie his lace as his dad spoke to Uncle Jim.

'Do a good job buttering this bread, Jim. Remember, dignity in the work process.'

Uncle Jim mumbled something under his breath that John couldn't hear.

*　　　　*　　　　*

John went out the back way to the shop. He walked past Jackie Ryan's old house and, before he knew what he was doing, he had pushed Jackie's yard door. He glanced at the corrugated tin sheets over the windows, and then the door moved. It wasn't locked; no one was around and John told himself he'd just have a quick look, then go to Elsie's.

He knew it was best to get into the empty houses as soon as the people moved out, before the houses were vandalised. Sometimes those who were moving never even got beyond the street before the kids were in. John would be one of them. He would wander around the empty house and think 'Flippin' hell they were having their tea here last night.'

He'd notice the marks on the linoleum from the table legs and would look out of the bedroom windows and see the street from a different angle. And look into other people's backyards.

Sometimes he would find magazines, comics, old toys, keys and books. But when he entered the Ryans' it was a mess. He'd been in once before, when Jackie's family first moved out a fortnight ago but John's mother found out, she smacked him and kept him in. Now other kids had been in and wrecked everything. They'd broken the windows and torn the wallpaper off, smashed the sink and someone had even had a crap in the corner. John guessed that older lads had been in, because the lead pipes that fed the sink had gone and the old lead light fittings had been ripped out. He'd heard that gangs were going around tearing out the lead from empty houses; sometimes they even took it from the roofs.

The Corporation had started moving people out from the far end of John's street a while before. All the houses there were empty and a few had been demolished. Now, the empty houses were closer to John's house, and whole streets of empty houses were a common sight. John's mother had told him that families who were due to be moved received three offers of a new house. John had often asked his mam when they might be moving, but she'd always said that they didn't have to move just because other people were moving.

He wandered around Jackie's house. He'd been in lots of times when Jackie lived there but now, he thought, it was a sad place. He went into the back bedroom, which Jackie's parents had used. He took a quick look out the window and then went to the front bedroom, the one that Jackie had shared with his younger brother, Danny, and the girls. John could picture where the two beds had been. He stood in the vandalised room and wondered who would be the first to go into his house if it became empty.

John looked at where the beds used to be, and shouted out, 'See ya Jackie, best of luck in your new house with your new school as well! Oh an' best of luck with your new mates!' He shouted louder, 'See ya! See ya Jackie!'

Then he turned towards the door and tossed the half-crown his dad had given him. He caught it in mid-air and wondered if Jackie would get into his new school's football team. He tossed the coin again, higher and, as it spun he heard a voice shout from the street.

'Who the bleedin' hell's that in there? If ya don't come out now I'm gonna call the police!'

John froze as the coin bounced on the floorboards.

'Oh soddin' hell,' he thought. 'It's Mr. Costello.'

He bent down quickly to pick up the half-crown and banged his head against the door, which slammed shut. He rubbed his head, then reached out to open the door and nearly shit himself: there was no doorknob. Someone had pinched the bleeding knob.

'Right, if you don't come out before I count to ten, that's your lot. One!'

John put his hand to the lock. He tried to jam his fingers in between the door and its frame, but it was hopeless. He pushed his finger into the slot where the handle's metal shaft had been, and tried to turn it, but nothing happened.

'Two!'

'Oh shit!' he thought. 'What I need is an lolly-ice stick.' He'd opened a door before by jamming a lolly-ice stick into the slot and turning it.

'Three!'

John looked around the room but all he saw was ripped-off wallpaper on the floor.

'Four!

He knew if he were caught there'd be no chance of going to see The Beatles. He stared around the room. He threw the wallpaper into one corner.

'Five!' Mike's dad continued his countdown.

John searched the floor, but there was no lolly-ice stick. There was nothing, just dust, the pile of wallpaper and pieces of plaster.

'Six!

'A lolly-ice stick, that's all, hey God,' said John. And then he began to say a Hail Mary.

'Seven!' shouted Mr Costello.

'I'll say ten Hail Mary's and ten Our Fathers for an lolly-ice stick, honest I will, I will,' said John.

'Eight!'

He moved back to the handle less door and knelt down.

'Nine!'

'Oh soddin' hell,' he thought. 'What'll my mam say? She'll tell my dad. Oh God, I wanna die.' He was on the verge of crying.

'Ten! Right! That's it. I'm goin' to get my belt.'

'Oh friggin' hell,' thought John, 'his belt's worse than the police.'

John frantically scanned the floor wild eyed, then he saw it: the skirting board had been pulled away. From his kneeling position he grabbed at the loose skirting board and pulled. It snapped. 'Bloody hell, did Mr. Costello hear that? No,' he told himself, 'he's gone inside for his belt that's good. How can that be good ya soft get,' John scolded himself. He bit into the broken piece of skirting board and it gave, but the piece was still too big. He bit into it again. It tasted horrible, but the wood cracked. He pulled at it and a small piece snapped off.

John pushed the wood into the hole where the handle had been, jammed it in, and turned. But it snapped and, swearing to himself and apologising to God at the same time, John pulled the broken bits from the hole in the door.

'Hey come out, ya robbers!'

John went cold. It was Mike, down in the street.

'Come out,' yelled Mike. 'My dad's gone to get his belt. It's a bleedin' big one, a big docker's belt, and he's gonna smack yer arse.'

John pushed the wood into the hole again and jammed it as tight as he could. He banged it with the palm of his hand, which hurt, but he wasn't bothered. He turned it very slowly and said another Hail Mary. He twisted the wood slowly and the latch began to move with it.

John knew he had to keep the latch turned and at the same time pull at the wood to open the door.

It worked.

The door opened and John flew from the room, not noticing that he was holding his breath. He went down the stairs three at a time and suddenly stopped – he remembered his dad's money: the half-crown. He turned and ran back, saw the coin, snatched it up, his heart thumping all the time, and wondered if you could have a heart attack when you were eleven. He didn't know.

When he was outside he ducked his head and ran all the way to Elsie's. There was another customer at the counter when he entered the shop, which gave him a chance to get his breath back. As he waited he banged dust off his trousers.

'A jar of crab paste and a jar of salmon paste, please Elsie.'

'Hello John. Been running?' asked Elsie.

'Yeah, er yeah. I'm in training for the school football team.'

'That's nice.' Elsie handed John the jars and he gave her the money.

'Are you sweating, John?' she asked suddenly.

'What?'

'I said it looks like you're sweating.'

'Oh. Am I?'

'No it's alright it's nothing; you're too young to sweat. There you go here's your change. Bye son.'

'Er, yeah,' he said. 'Thanks Elsie.'

He left the shop as quickly as he could. Outside the shop he thought, ' What does that mean, you're too young to sweat?' John put his finger across his forehead it was wet. He held his finger up, 'Yis sweat. There y'are Elsie what's that, I should think so. I was like bleedin' James Bond in there.'

When John arrived home James Bond nearly got battered.

His mother shouted, 'Where have you been? I only sent you to the shop for the paste, not the place where they make it!'

His dad said, 'The state of you! You're rotten, your hands are filthy.'

And Uncle Jim said, 'Ah, hey lad, where have you been with the grub? I'm starving.'

John suddenly felt like Goldilocks with the three bears. He nearly laughed thinking about it. But he managed not to.

'Get that shirt off and put this one on,' his mother half-shouted. 'It looks like you've been down the mines. What's that dirty mark around your mouth?'

'I fell over, mam. I must have had dirt on my hands and rubbed my face.'

'What took you so long?'

'Er, er, I met this lad from school. We were talking about this afternoon, about going to see The Beatles.'

'Are you telling lies, John?'

'I can't tell lies, can I mam? I go to Church.'

'Don't you be cheeky to your mam, lad, or I'll give you a smack,' said his dad. 'Give yourself a wash. You look a disgrace.'

John washed his hands. Uncle Jim smiled and John wasn't sure if he was smiling because he thought it was funny, or because he was going to be fed.

'There's your change, dad.'

'Thanks, son.'

John sat down at the table and picked up a sandwich. And then he remembered he hadn't taken his thre'pence.

He said, 'Er, I didn't take that thre'pence for going to Elsie's, dad, you know because... you're not working today, are you?'

His dad smiled and looked at his mother and at Uncle Jim.

'That's very considerate of you,' said Uncle Jim, with a large grin, 'very considerate.'

Uncle Jim turned to John's dad. 'That's what I was talking about before, Tom. Fraternity. Solidarity. Got to stick together.' He turned back to John. 'Smashing that, lad.'

John sat there with a gob on. Uncle Jim didn't get it. He wanted to say, 'I only said that, Uncle Jim; I don't want to know about your fraternity or your solidarity, whatever they are. I want my thre'pence back... ah sod it.'

'You be careful when you go up there, lad,' his mother said. 'It was on the wireless about The Beatles. They said there'll be thousands of youngsters there. And John, before you go, change your trousers; they look dirty. Put your dungarees on.'

'The zip's broke, mam; it keeps on coming down.'

'It doesn't matter. Put a pin in it.' Then she looked at his shoes. 'And give your shoes a polish; they make you look scruffy. I don't know what you do in them shoes, lad. Use your old ones for football.'

'I haven't been playing football in them.'

'Well you've been doing something in them.'

'But Kathleen,' said his dad, 'he's only going to watch The Beatles, he's not going to get up on the stage and sing with them. Who'll see his shoes? You said yourself there'll be thousands there. They're not all going up there to see our John's shoes.'

Uncle Jim laughed.

'Don't talk daft. Do you know why you're saying that? Working with him!' His mother had her arms folded but she moved one arm under the other, pointed a finger at her brother and spoke to her husband, 'You'll end up as daft as him if you're not careful. The sooner he gets moved into another gang on the docks, the better.'

'Ah don't be like that, Kathleen,' said Uncle Jim. 'And anyway, Tom's right; who'll see the lad's shoes?'

'I don't care, Jim; you're a bad influence, you, and I'm not sending the lad out where all those people are with his shoes dirty. What if he had an accident?'

'Oh I see, in case the Saint John's Ambulance man wants to give his feet the kiss of life.'

John's dad burst out laughing. Uncle Jim did the same.

'You're soft, the both of you; just listen to yourselves. You're like a pair of kids.' His mother went to the sink and filled the kettle.

*   *   *

In his bedroom John took his trousers off and saw dirt on the back that he hadn't noticed before. He told himself he should have dusted himself down properly before he came back into the house. He'd have to remember that next time he went into a bomdie.

He collected all the money he'd hidden away and counted it. He had one and sixpence, but Billy wanted five bob. Five bob would be worth it to have a really good look at The Beatles; he might even be seen on the television. Everybody would want to know him then. He put on his dungarees, and took a pin out his pocket, as he looked at the pictures of The Beatles on the wall, and then he went into his mother's bedroom.

A picture of the Sacred Heart of Jesus hung over the dresser. John opened the top drawer of the dresser and saw what he knew would be there. Mary had sent him on errands to the shops and told him where to get the money before now. He emptied the purse onto the dresser and counted the money: one pound, six shillings and tuppence. John reasoned that he could borrow the money: he would tell Mary to pay it back from his pocket money.

'Borrowing's not stealing,' he told himself as he counted out the three shillings and sixpence he needed. 'Borrowing's not stealing.'

Then he put the rest of the money back in the purse and stared at the three shillings and sixpence.

But if he were stealing, he would tell the priest in confession. The priest would give him ten Hail Mary's and ten Acts of Contrition, but he could do them in no time. It would be worth it... to see The Beatles, to really see them.

John looked up.

He stood perfectly still, staring at the Sacred Heart of Jesus above him. Then he glanced in the mirror, but he couldn't look at himself. He pushed the coins he'd counted out back into the purse and shut the drawer.

His mother's voice made him jump. She was shouting at him to hurry up.

John called back, 'Er, I can't find a pin for my zip.'

'Come down, I've got one here,' said his mother, her voice softer.

'Alright.'

John took the pin out of his zip, shoved it in his pocket and went downstairs.

'Here's a pin,' said his mother.

'Ta.'

'And your shoes John, don't forget your shoes.'

In the parlour John took the shoebox from the sideboard and sat on the couch.

Peter came through the front door. 'Alright?' he said, 'You still here, then? I thought you'd be up there by now getting a good spec. Better hurry.'

'I am. But I'm polishing my shoes first.'

'Ah well, you've got to look the part with all them girls up there, don't ya? Or you won't cop off.'

John blushed. 'I'm not going there for girls, to cop off. I'm just going to see The Beatles.'

Peter looked at him, straight-faced. 'Then why are you polishing your shoes?'

'Because my mam told me to!'

'Alright, alright, keep your hair on.' Peter shook his head and sang, 'Yeah, yeah, yeah.' Peter disappeared into the kitchen.

John smiled as he put polish on the brush. He heard Peter mention the new wallpaper as he washed his hands at the sink.

'How did the meeting go?' said Uncle Jim.

'You know,' said Peter, 'the same. Union official said it's alright. They'll sort it out for us.'

'I'm sure they'll sort it out; sort us out at the same time. Wouldn't trust that lot as far as I could throw them.'

'Bit unfair that, isn't it Jim?' said John's dad.

'Well, we're all entitled to our own opinion but that's what I think. Some of the full-time officials for the T an' G are more right-wing than the soddin' Monday Club.'

'The who?'

'Doesn't matter. But look times are changing. There's going to be more stacker trucks, more forklift trucks and more cranes on the docks. There's got to be, it's a nap.' Uncle Jim sighed. 'If we don't start acting now we're going to get it in the neck. It's bad enough now, but when these changes really start, watch what'll happen. And the T an' G know this; so do the Dock Labour Board, and you can bet your bottom dollar the bosses do as well. All jolly good friends together, they are.'

'You can't stop progress, Jim,' said John's dad. 'More stacker trucks and the likes can only make our jobs better. As you said, the times are changing.'

'I know that, I know that, but what's going to happen to the lads still working there? Are they going to get better pay, better conditions, regular work instead of going into the pens every morning and getting a tap on the shoulder? I'm not against change, Tom; I'm all for change, provided we're involved in the change; provided we get some benefit out of the change.'

'The thing is, dad,' said Peter, 'it's about ownership of what's down there. The important thing is the ownership of the economic means of production, like the factories, the ships and the quays and warehouses.'

John looked up and saw the back of his mother's head in the cabinet mirror in the doorway. She shook her head, fast.

'I'm not interested in all that, son,' said John's dad.

'I don't believe my ears!' said John's mother. 'You've turned our Peter into a communist, you and your mates in that Star Club.'

'What are you talking about, Kathleen? I haven't turned him into anything. Anyway what's a communist?' said Uncle Jim.

'Someone who doesn't believe in God and lives in Russia?

What about those who are communists but live in China? Aren't they real communists?'

'Yes.'

'What about someone in London who's a communist; is he a real communist?'

'Yes.'

'So it's nothing to do with the place is it? It's just an idea. So why don't you like the idea, because it goes against the Catholic faith?'

'Yes - they're not Catholics; they don't know the truth.'

'What's the truth? What you read in the Catholic Pic' or the Universe, or what Father Bunloaf tells you and the rest of them.'

'Oh that's blasphemy, that! Oh, God forgive ya. You want to tell that to the priest in confession.'

'You're joking, aren't you? The only time I'm near a priest is when I'm in the pub and he's getting free ale.'

'I'll tell you what, Jim Mulhearn; you'll go to hell the way you're carrying on.

'I think I'm already there, girl. I wish I had the price of a pint.'

'Oh, so you want to go the pub now? Not content with causing murder down the docks and not doing any work, you want to go to the pub. Why don't you go home and see your wife? Poor woman.'

'*Poor woman?*'

'Yes. Poor woman. She must be, married to you,' said John's mother. 'And anyway, if you're so clever, where would you rather live? America or Russia?'

Uncle Jim held the teapot, but he hadn't poured any tea out. He put it down.

'You got me there, Kath,' he said. 'If you had loads of money, if you were a millionaire, then maybe America's the best place for you. But if you need a job, or help when you're sick, then Russia. You think Russia's bad because you've read it in the papers. But in Russia women get treated just like men, have the same rights as men and everything. Like if you went over to Russia you'd be equal to Tom. But then again I suppose that'd be a step down for you.'

John saw his mother turn her head quickly towards Uncle Jim, but he couldn't see her face.

It went quiet. John sat with one hand inside his shoe, holding the brush in the other. He hadn't even begun polishing.

'John! John!' shouted his mother, suddenly. 'Are you still there?'

He pushed himself back into the couch in case she saw his reflection in the cabinet mirror.

'Er, yeah, my lace has snapped,' he said. 'Just fixing it, then I'm going.'

He'd been copped ear-wigging. He gave his shoes a quick polish and thought about the time Uncle Jim had told him the story of *Spartacus*, about slaves fighting the Romans for their freedom. It helped him understand what Uncle Jim had been talking about in the kitchen. But he didn't say anything.

'Going to see them, now?' called Uncle Jim.

'He's going nowhere. Not until I've had a word with Steve Costello and the Dunleavy lads.' His mother's voice had an edge to it. She glared at Uncle Jim when she spoke.

'He'll be alright,' Uncle Jim said, pretending to play a guitar.

'It's nothing to do with you, Jim Mulhearn, so keep your opinions to yourself.' Again she glared at her brother. Then she said, 'So go and get Steve and the twins, John; I want to have a word.'

'Er, I'm not going with Steve or the twins. It's me, Mike and Billy Mogan.'

'But Billy Mogan's only the same age as you.'

'He's six months older than me. He's one of the oldest lads in our year.'

'No, John, you can't go with them.'

'It's alright, mam. Billy Mogan used to live up by Princes Road. It's alright.'

'It's not alright, John. You're not going!'

'Hey, Kath,' said Uncle Jim.

'And you can stay out of it,' said John's mother.

'Kath, the lad's only going to Princes Road.'

'Keep out of it. Star Club indeed. He's not going.'

'Mam, mam,' shouted John, suddenly. 'That's not fair! I'm not a kid! It's not *friggin' fair*!'

'That's enough, John! Get to your room!'

John ran up the stairs and sat on his bed. He heard his mother and Uncle Jim arguing downstairs. He heard Uncle Jim say, 'He's old enough.' And he heard his mother say, 'He's not your lad.'

And then John heard the men leave through the backyard. He heard Uncle Jim say to his dad, 'Go back in and have a word for the lad.'

'It's a waste of time, Jim,' said John's dad.

John heard the backyard door close, and then he sat on the edge of the bed and waited, for what he didn't know.

He heard his mother tidying up downstairs.

He looked at the pictures of the Beatles.

He said, loudly, 'I'm not a kid' as he opened the wardrobe and took out Peter's jacket.

He put it on, turned the collar to the inside and turned the cuffs up.

He combed his hair down, and with a pair of scissors cut his fringe.

He stood in front of the mirror and listened as his mother switched on the radio and put the dishes in the sink.

He buttoned the jacket up, pushed the window up with his fingertips, climbed out onto the window ledge and stretched over to the drainpipe.

Chapter Eight
GOING

Liverpool is where the Irish came when they ran out of
potatoes, and it's where black people were left behind as
slaves or whatever. We were a great amount of Irish
descent and blacks and Chinamen all sorts.

John Lennon, 1964

John stood outside Mike's door, his head half-turned toward
his own house as he shouted through the letterbox.   Mike   came
out.

'You're not half late. I was just gonna call for you.'

John looked at him.

'What?'

'I said, you're late - you should have called ages ago.'

'No, I mean what's that?'

Mike was wearing a large, bright yellow jumper. It looked
to be on back to front.

'What's what?'

'That! What you've got on?'

Mike looked down. 'It's a jumper. What does it look like;
are you soft?'

'Whose is it?'

'It's mine! Whose d'ya think?'

John stared. *Am I soft*? He thought. But instead said,
'Whose is it?'

'It's mine. It was our Brenda's. Remember I told you about the telly cameras being up there, well you have to wear something different, something that'll make you stand out.'

'Soddin' hell - you'll stand out in that, Mike,' said John. 'As a matter of fact you'll be lucky if you don't get locked up. Taken away to the loony bin.'

'You won't be saying that when I'm on the telly and your not.'

Mike stared at John. Then he smiled. 'I like the hair and your coat.'

'Yeah.' John glanced down at Peter's jacket. 'Come on, let's hurry up.' He turned towards his house, ready to run if he had to.

The boys approached Billy's Auntie's. John glanced at Mike's jumper. It was swimming on him and there were two small holes where the elbows used to be. John couldn't help but admire Mike's cheek.

'Know what happened before?' asked Mike

'What?'

'Well,' Mike paused for effect, 'there was a gang of robbers in the Ryans' house. They were going to get into our house through Ryans' loft. Remember, like we did at the top end of the street when we knocked through the walls?'

'It wasn't us who did that was it, Mike? It was the older lads in the gang, and your Steve's mates.'

'Yeah, but we climbed through, didn't we? Remember?'

'Yeah, we climbed through and got rotten, full of soot.' Steve and some older lads had climbed into the loft of an empty house and made a hole through the dividing wall and through to three other houses that were still occupied. Steve bragged that he saw a couple 'shaggin' although John guessed it was a lie. And the next day Mike included himself as one who'd also seen the couple.

'Yeah, well, anyway,' said Mike, 'this was better; these were robbers. They were trying to do the same as us, only break in.

My dad heard them. I did too. I heard one of the robbers shoutin' to his mate, "Blackie! Blackie! I've found some lead." My dad went out and shouted, "Come out ya bastards. I'll kill yas!" Me dad was gonna kill them. It was great.'

'How many was there?'

'Er… ' Mike counted on his fingers.

John thought he must be as daft as Mike for asking.

'Er, I think... about four,' was the number Mike finally decided on.

'How do you know?'

'We seen them leg it over the Billy 'ock, they were big. They were men.'

John was fed up with Mike's lies and before he could stop himself he blurted out.

'Maybe they just wanted to get in to hear your mam and dad having a shag.'

'What?'

John couldn't believe what he'd said.

Mike stopped. 'What'd you say that for?' he said.

John was scared. He didn't want to get into a fight when he knew he was in the wrong. They walked along for a while in silence. John hoped Mike wasn't going to sulk. They came to the end of the street and stood opposite Billy's Auntie's.

'Shall I whistle? Or shall we go up?' said John.

'Up to you. I'm not bothered.' Mike looked down and straightened the bottom of his jumper.

John whistled and then glanced at Mike, who immediately turned away. He was in a sulk.

'Maybe he's in the front room and can't hear us,' said John. 'Come on Mike, let's give him a knock.'

John pushed open the letterbox and called in. Mike leaned over the handrail and looked down the stairwell.

At last Billy came out. He looked at John's hair and coat and at Mike's jumper, then at John again. 'Bleedin' 'ell,' he said, 'is the circus in town?'

Mike didn't look up.

'You're late,' said Billy. 'I thought you weren't gonna come. Better hurry up then.' Billy closed the door and went down the stairs.

John followed.

'You're not the leader! You're not the boss!' shouted Mike.

John and Billy stopped.

'What's up with him?' said Billy, as he turned around.

'Ah nothing,' said John. 'Come on Mike, we're gonna be late. We won't get a good spec.'

Mike followed them, slowly, down the stairs.

John said, 'You know what you were saying about the five bob, Billy, for the spec?'

'I was only kidding,' said Billy. 'I know a good place to watch from. You didn't believe me about wanting five bob did ya?'

'Er. No, no,' lied John, looking at Billy. 'Where is it?'

'Top of Upper Stanny.'

'Where?' asked Mike.

'Princes Road, there's a church with steps going up to it. There's a stone wall around the steps. Should be able to get a good look from there. Maybe stand on the wall if you want to.'

'That sounds good, doesn't it, Mike?' said John. 'If we're on the wall and the cameras are there you might be on the telly tonight with yer jumper.'

'Yeah, that's good that. Yeah, high on a wall,' said Mike.

'What?' said Billy.

'Mike's wearing the jumper so he'll get on telly.'

'Is that what he's wearing it for? I thought it was for a bet.'

'Get lost, you, Mogan,' Mike half-shouted.

They walked outside the block and Billy said, 'It's on back to front.'

'No it's not,' said Mike. 'It's just different; it used to be a V-neck an' now it's a crew neck, that's all.'

'Whose was it?'

'Their Brenda give it him,' John replied.

'Well give it back to her,' said Billy.

Mike glared at him. Billy slowly looked Mike up and down.

'Turn around, Mike.'

Mike didn't move.

'Go on, turn around. What are you scared of?'

Mike reluctantly and slowly turned around.

'I thought it was a girl's - there's two lumps in the back.'

'Fuck off you, Mogan!' Mike spun back around.

But Billy carried on, 'You'll have to watch it when we get up there, y'know, someone might try and shag you.'

The boys walked.

John wanted to laugh. If he did, Mike would have gone home, definitely. Billy knew he'd gone too far. Mike stepped two paces behind them so the back of his jumper couldn't be seen.

'What's with the hair?' Billy asked John, quietly.

'What?'

'The hair? The state of it. And the jacket?'

'Mike said he liked it - and the jacket.'

'John, he's got an excuse,' Billy nodded behind at Mike. 'He's cracked.'

John glanced back at Mike and his jumper. Then he ruffled his fringe and took Peter's jacket off. He hung it on a railing outside a house and convinced himself and Billy it was too hot for a coat anyway.

'How long did you live up by Prinny Road for, then?' asked John.

'Dunno, since I was a kid. We lived in a flat, then the Corpy got us a house where we are now.'

'It's not a real house though, is it, with a backyard like ours?' said Mike.

'No it's not a real house, Mike, you're right there,' Billy agreed without conviction.

'Did you like it up there?' asked John.

'Yeah, it was alright; wasn't bad. But because it was a flat we had to share a lavatory and the bathroom with the others in the flats.'

Yuck! That's shit, that is,' said Mike.

'Wasn't that bad. Anyway, look at you. Your houses are old; that's why they're getting knocked down. You've only got an outside lav', just one tap, and you've only got a tin bath, so what's the difference?'

Mike stopped and fixed his eyes on Billy.

'Yeah, but at least I know whose arse has been on our lav! And anyway that's now, but we're moving, see - going to the outskirts, to Halewood - Maggots Lane! Gonna have four bedrooms. Me and our Steve's gonna have one between us, fuckin' big back garden and a garden in the front,' Mike's voice rose with every word. 'Brand new house! Toilet inside and a bathroom, hot water, everything brand bleedin' new - what d'ya think of that!'

John felt as if he'd been punched in the stomach. Mike was leaving the street, going to the outskirts, and he might not see him after he'd left. He felt awful, empty. Mike was leaving, and he had never said anything to him. Then he thought, 'You sod.'

'You never told me, sly arse,' said John.

'Er, er... my mam never knew till this week. She, said, "Don't tell anyone".'

'Well you've just told soddin' us, haven't ya?'

John felt awful; empty. First Jackie Ryan, now Mike. There'd be no one left to play with soon. No gang left. No street left.

'Ah sod it,' he said. 'Maggot's bloody Lane, what a stupid soddin' name.'

Mike ignored John and said, 'Should we cut across the Hollow?' The Hollow was a large empty space, covered with grit, which rose sharply from the street below it. The kids called it Biddy Hill because of the steepness of the incline. Every November for a week, a travelling fair arrived and set up there. At the bottom of the incline stood a large electric sub-station, forty foot high, its

111

top standing a few feet higher than the plateau of the Hollow. The kids in the neighbourhood called the sub-station Chocky Island.

The boys dug their feet into the grit mound and climbed. Mike pointed to Chocky Island and said, to Billy, 'See that, there's loads of caseys and footballs up there, you know? It looks flat on top doesn't it? But it's not. There's a little wall all around on top but you can't tell from here. I've seen loads of lads playing footy up on the Hollow and seen the ball get kicked on top of Chocky Island, loads of times. Our Steve's been on top of there, you know?' He climbed up the drainpipe.'

John looked at the sub-station and at the square, cast-iron drainpipes, set flush within the brickwork.

'Yeah, our Steve found loads of balls: caseys, Fridos, all kinds,' declared Mike.

'What did he do with them?' asked Billy.

'Er, gave me some and gave some to his mates and, er, some were burst.'

'I don't remember you having any footballs from there,' said John.

'I, er, took them to school and swapped them for some toy soldiers and comics.'

'Why do they call it Chocky Island?' asked Billy.

'Don't know,' said Mike. 'The little kids sing a song, "Row, row, row to Choc... ky Is... land." That's all I know.'

John knew the tune was from "McNamara's Band". His Uncle Jim and his mother sang the song at parties. He would have mentioned it but he couldn't be bothered. *Maggot's soddin' Lane*.

'Hey, John, remember when the fair used to come round? It was great, wasn't it?' said Mike

'A fair comes here?' asked Billy.

'Oh, yeah, doesn't it, John? It comes when the dark nights are here. It's great, isn't it, John?'

John knew Mike was trying to get around him because he was moving out of the street. But John didn't reply. 'Sod him,' he thought.

But Mike carried on. 'It comes here every year. Dodgems and shooting ducks, coconut shy, merry-go-round with the horses on, stacks of rides an' that, isn't there John?'

'Yeah stacks,' replied John sarcastically.

'We'd climb under the waltzers and find loads of money that the people had lost when they'd been on the rides. Me and John found loads. Once we found a ten bob note, didn't we?'

'I don't remember that!'

'Oh, er, I think I was with our Steve then, but we used to find loads of money, didn't we?'

'Yeah loads of friggin' a'pennies.'

Billy laughed. The boys had reached level ground.

'Ah, we found more than them,' continued Mike. 'Remember, we used to get a chase off Albie McInerney. He used to think he was a big boss when the fair came, keeping all the kids away from the dodgems and the waltzers. We used to call him to get a chase. It was a laugh, wasn't it?'

John didn't answer. He just looked at Billy, who had taken something out of his pocket and put it into his mouth. 'What you doing, Billy?' said John.

'Lightin' up. What's it look like?' He bent down and struck a match on half a brick.

'Don't be doing that.'

'Why?'

'Why? Say someone sees us?'

'It's not you, is it?'

'But I'm with you.'

'Yeah, but you're not smoking, are ya? I am.'

'Yeah but, yeah... but they don't know that, so they might think I'm smoking as well.'

'Who will?'

'The ones who see us.'

'Who?'

'Anyone.'

'No one will see us. Look, I'll hide it.' Billy took a drag and held the cigarette with his finger and thumb so it was covered inside his hand. 'And I'll bend down when I take a drag, don't worry. It'll be alright. It's not you, is it?'

'Bleedin' hell, I hope no one sees us,' John muttered in despair. 'I'll get soddin' murdered.'

'See over there, Billy?' Mike stopped and pointed. 'The back of that bombed shop?'

'It just looks like a bomdie to me,' said Billy.

'Well it was a bleedin' shop.' Mike glared at Billy. 'Anyway, we found some lead in the backyard, didn't we John? And we melted it down, didn't we?'

'Your Steve and his mate from school did.'

'Yeah, well, we were with them, weren't we? We were there. Our Steve found some old lead pipe and we got some wood and made a fire. Then we put the lead in. And we melted it down.'

'What for?' asked Billy.

'I'll tell you now, what we did was we got bricks, right, good clean ones, ones that had smooth sides on them, and we put them together like to make a… what was it, John?'

'A mould.'

'That's it, a mould. Yeah, four bricks on a slate, and we put grass sods and bits of wood outside on the corners so the lead wouldn't leak out. And when the lead was boiling hot we'd put it in the, er, mould. Then we'd let it get cold, yeah. Then we took all the bricks away.'

'And what happened then?' asked Billy.

'What was it like, John? It was great wasn't it? Great! It was like a brick of heavy lead. And know what we did then?'

'What?'

'We pissed on it.'

'Pissed on it! What for?'

'What for? So we could polish it up, to make it look shiny. It was like a gold lead brick.'

'A what?' Billy looked at them, his eyes wide. Then he shook his head and laughed.

John felt soft.

'Yeah it was good; great,' said Mike. Billy stopped laughing.

'Dead good; great,' mimicked Billy and laughed again.

Mike never picked up on Billy's tease. 'Yeah it was, wasn't it John?'

Billy pointed at Mike. 'What did you polish it up with? Not your jumper?'

'No, don't be daft. I don't remember, but it was great, wasn't it John?'

John hung his head and kicked at the grit. 'The quicker this soft sod moves to Halewood the better,' he thought.

Billy put his arm out straight and flicked his ciggy stump away.

John's shoulders sagged as he looked at Mike and Billy. 'I'm going to see The, soddin', Beatles with Wild Willie Woodbine and the Mad Custard,' he thought.

The boys walked in silence until Mike spoke to Billy.

'So do you know loads of lads up here, then?'

'Yeah, I know a few - why?'

'Just asking. What school did you used to go to?'

'St Bernard's.'

'Doesn't sound Catholic, that. Are ya a prodessan?'

'What?'

'A proddy dog.'

'No, I'm not a prod-ee-dog, I'm a Cat-o-lic.'

'He must be a Catholic, mustn't he Mike, if he goes to Saint Pat's?'

'Oh yeah, I forgot,' replied Mike.

'Anyway, I don't know what you two are going on about,' said Billy. 'Catholic, Protestant; it's all a load of shite. All that going to Church, all that mumbo jumbo Latin stuff; daft.'

'Well why do you go to Church then?' asked John.

'That's it John, I don't. Our Sheila and Patty try to make me go; I just leave the house and hang around the street and say I've been. They try to trip me up asking what colour the priest's vestments were and that. I just say green or purple, change them round - they don't know 'cause they don't go themselves - all them saints days when you have a day off school, Holy Days of Obildeegobbildy; just daft.'

'They're Holy Days of Obligation them,' said Mike.

'I know that, Mike, I used to go with my mam.'

'How long's your mam been dead?'

John couldn't believe Mike.

'I don't know.'

They walked along for a while, saying nothing.

'Here y'are. I've got a joke for ya,' said Billy. ' Listen to this. There's this lad and he's late for school and when he gets into the classroom the teacher says, "Where have you been, Johnny?" And he says, "I've been to the pond, Miss, catching frogs." She says, "Catching frogs?" "Yes, Miss," he says. "And when we catch them we put a straw up their arse and blow them right up." Then Miss says, "Johnny, don't you mean rectum?" "Rectum? Miss, we blew them to friggin' bits".'

Billy bent over and laughed loudly. John looked at Mike, who looked as puzzled as John. He didn't get the joke either. When Billy stopped laughing John and Mike told him they didn't get it, so Billy explained.

But John still didn't think it was funny. 'Fancy doing that to a poor frog,' he thought.

They stopped near to a pub.

'You know Biddy Hill?' said Billy. 'Why do they call it Biddy Hill?'

'My Uncle Jim says it's not Biddy, but Bibby,' said John.

'Bibby? What's that?' said Billy.

'It was a factory on the Dock Road, at the bottom of Hill Street. It got bombed in the war.'

'So what's that got to do with it?' demanded Mike.

'Well I'm telling you, aren't I? Bibby's was bombed and the Corpy never had time to move all the bricks, so they pushed them all together and left it 'till they could move them after the war. It was piled really high and they used to call it Bibby's Hill. That's why the kids call where we've just been Biddy Hill because of Bibby's Hill. The kids got it mixed up. That's what Uncle Jim said, anyway.'

'Nar, that's soft that,' said Mike. 'It's Biddy Hill! Everyone knows that. All the kids know that. Anyway, what does your Uncle Jim know? He doesn't live round here.'

'He used to live round here,' said John and he felt his face burning. He wanted to give Mike a bleedin' good punch.

'John sounds right to me,' said Billy. 'Bibby's Hill, yeah, because anyway what's biddies? That's what you get in your hair, isn't it, when you have to get a biddy comb or stuff in a bottle for nits.'

'That's what I mean! That's what I'm saying,' said Mike. 'See all the muck and all the grit and that on Biddy Hill; the kids play on it, don't they? And when they play on it they make dust.' He banged his jumper with his hands for effect. 'So the dust and muck gets in their hair, see.' He scratched his hair. 'And that's what happens; they get biddies in their hair. That's why they call it Biddy Hill. So ya wrong!'

John looked at his best mate. 'Flippin' 'eck, Mike,' he thought, 'I'm going to have to say a prayer for you tonight when I go to bed. You're going soft in the bleedin' head.'

*   *   *

They came to May Brennan's shop. John felt in his pockets.

'I've got some money - you know, we can go into May's and buy some sweets.'

'Yeah alright, great,' said Mike. 'How much have you got?' John gave him a look. *You're nice to me now, you miserable get.*

'How much have you got?' asked Mike again.

'I don't know, I'll have to look.'

'Will you buy us a loosey?' said Billy.

'What? I'm not buying you ciggies Billy, get lost.'

'I don't want you to get me ciggies, just one.'

'No!'

'Why?'

'That's why!'

'Why's that?'

'My mam would kill me.'

'Your mam's not here.'

'I know that.'

'So how will she find out?'

'I don't know... but she might.'

'How?'

'I don't know.'

'Alright then, give me the money an' I'll buy one myself.'

'No!'

'Why?'

'That's why.'

'I won't smoke it now; I'll wait till we get up there.'

'No.'

'You're tight you, John.'

'I'm not. Anyway look, if I go in the shop with you and you're getting a loosey, then May or Joe will know I'm with you.'

'So?'

'So, me and my mam go in there after Church sometimes an' May might tell her.'

'Alright then, I'll go in first. You wait outside.'

'No.'

'Why?'

'Because it's not right; it's wrong.'

'What is?'

'You, smoking; you're too young. It's bad for you, everyone knows that. Don't they, Mike?'

'What?' said Mike.

'I said, smoking's bad for you.'

'But your mam smokes, John, and your Mary and so does my mam an' dad; loads do.'

'Yeah, but it's still bad for you.'

'Anyway, how much have you got?'

'Soddin' hell Mike, I've just told you I don't know. I'll have to count it.'

John was sorry he'd opened his bleeding mouth now about going to May's. Mike and Billy were driving him around the bend.

'So you gonna buy me one then?' persisted Billy.

'Don't you know,' he said, 'that you'd just be making a show of yourself.'

'What do you mean?'

'They won't serve you, May or Joe.'

'They will.'

'They won't; none of the kids that go to our school have ever got ciggies from May's, not even if they buy a packet of five or ten and say it's for their mam. They would get in trouble - it's too near to Saint Pats.'

'You sure?'

'Yeah! Here ya are, tell me this; who'd you know that's bought ciggies from May Brennan's shop?'

Mike tugged at John's shirtsleeve, 'How much have you got?'

'Oh fuck off, Mike,' said John under his breath. 'Come on, let's go in.'

When they were inside the shop John went through the motion of counting his money, 'Nine pence, ten pence, eleven pence, a shilling, one an' two, one and six.'

'How much is that each?' said Mike.

John stared at Mike, gobsmacked. *The bleedin' cheeky, greedy, hard faced sod!* 'Who said I was wackin' it out? I might just wanna let you pick something out or give you thre'pence.'

'Oh.'

There y'are, that shut you up.

He did share it out. Joe asked the boys were they going to see The Beatles and told them to look after themselves as they left. Joe was alright, even if he did look at Mike's jumper funny.

The boys waited to cross Park Place. Saint Patrick's Church faced them.

'Do you know there's priests buried in the Church grounds there?' said John.

'What are they buried there for?' asked Mike.

'Cause they're dead,' said Billy.

'Ah, funny!'

'How many priests are there?'

'Eleven,' said John and he pointed. 'See that stone cross in the front of the Church? Well that has all the names of the priests who died; there's three from Saint Pat's.'

'Why would you bury them there?'

'I don't really know. My mam told me. It was about a hundred years ago. Loads of people that were really poor came over from Ireland. Thousands and thousands of them and lots of them died. They caught diseases. It sounded really sad the way my mam was telling me.'

'What about the priests? What happened to them?' asked Mike.

'I'm telling you. All these people were dying of diseases and they had to have a priest to give them extreme unction - you know, the last rites - hear their confession and that. Where the poor people lived was overcrowded, in cellars and places like that, dozens of them. And when you go to confession no one's supposed to know what your sins are, only the priest, yeah?'

'Yeah.'

'So the man or the woman's dying and the priest has to get right down next to them so others in the room can't hear their confession. But the priest gets that close hearing the confession, he catches the disease off the one that's dying and he dies.'

'That's a good story, that,' said Mike.

'It's not a soddin' story. It happened, ya soft get.'

'No I didn't mean that, I meant... it's interesting.'

'*Interesting*,' said Billy. 'That's a new one for you, isn't it – interesting?' He turned to John. 'Is that true?'

'Yeah. Come on, let's cross the road. I think you can see the door to where they're buried on the other side.'

They crossed over to the Church.

'At the bottom, there's steps going down. That's called a crypt, that. That's where they're buried. See, Saint Pat's was the biggest Church around here. It was that big they had to split the parish up. See that,' said John pointing up at the cross on top of the Church wall above the statue of Saint Patrick. 'That's the first time in Liverpool that a cross could be shown outside a Catholic Church. My mam told me that a hundred years ago they wouldn't let any Catholic Churches show anyone that they were Catholic by having a cross outside; Saint Pat's was the first in Liverpool.'

'And see the statue of Saint Patrick,' said Mike. 'Well you can see one of his fingers is missing. See?' Mike pointed. 'The Orangemen pulled that off with a rope, after they had a march on the 12th of July.'

'I don't know about that, Mike,' said John. 'I never heard that one. Who said that?'

'Our Steve.'

Steve, again but John didn't say anything because he didn't want Mike going into another sulk. He just looked up at the eight-foot high statue of Saint Patrick in his green vestments and green and gold mitre, holding a staff. There was a carving of a shamrock under the statue that stood on a plinth. It was fifty foot high and John couldn't see anyone throwing a rope that far. But all he said to Mike was, 'You know tonight, after The Beatles get to the Town Hall, they're gonna have their dinner with the Lord Mayor. Then they're going to the Odeon to see the film that they've just made, *A Hard Day's Night*.'

'Yeah!'

'But all the tickets for the film have gone.'

'Yeah, I know.'

'Well my uncle says he knows a fella who works at the Odeon, on the door. He says if you give him two bob the fella will let you in for nothing.'

'Will he? Will he?' Mike shouted excited. 'Let you in for nothing if ya give him two bob. That's great.'

John and Billy burst out laughing.

'What are you laughing at?' said Mike. 'What's funny?'

Uncle Jim had caught John out with that one a few days before. John knew Mike would fall for it too.

They walked on for a while Mike and Billy ahead of John, until they were near the playground of Saint Patrick's Girls' School. Suddenly Mike shouted.

'Hear this, John,' said Mike, turning round and waiting for John to catch up. 'Billy's saying he went with a girl and they had a shag.'

John's mouth dropped open.

'You're a liar you, Billy Mogan,' shouted Mike. 'A bleeding liar. Do you think I'm daft? As if you did, as if.'

'Listen, just because you don't know how to do it doesn't mean others don't,' said Billy.

'Whatcha mean? Whatcha mean? I know! I know! I've heard our Steve and the others talking, I'm not soft.'

'Go on then,' Billy said. 'Tell me.'

'Why?'

'Because you don't know, that's why.'

'Alright! Alright! I'll tell ya. You get a girl, right... then you kiss her.'

Billy's eyes were wide open and his lips were pressed tightly together as he stared at Mike. John knew Billy was forcing himself not to laugh.

'And when you kiss 'er,' Mike continued, 'you kiss her for a bit like... and when you kiss her, your willy goes on pop an'... '

Billy tripped and fell off the kerb, laughing. John watched, mesmerised.

'Ah, fuck off - fuck off, Billy Mogan,' said Mike. 'Think ya smart, think you're big. Ya bl... bla... bleedin' sod.'

John thought he was going to say something else, and by the look on Billy's face so did he.

'I was only joking,' said Billy. 'You're right, I never did.'

'I knew you was only joking,' said Mike. 'So was I.'

They opened their bags of sweets and swapped, and then they walked over to Saint Martin's. The playground to the side of the school was full of builders' cabins.

'We've been up here, haven't we John, to watch the Js and the Shines fighting?' said Mike.

John spun round. He couldn't believe Mike had just said that in front of Billy. He hissed, 'Bleedin' hell, what did you say that for?' But Mike looked blank, as if he hadn't spoken.

'What was it like?' asked Billy, calmly.

'Well, er, it wasn't bad,' said John. 'Alright, y'know.' But he felt daft. 'Well, we'd come up and just sit on the wall and watch.'

'I used to watch as well,' said Billy. 'But from the other side of the school, the other side of Windsor Street.'

'I never saw you,' said Mike.

'Funny, I never saw you neither. Do you know why they called them the Js and the Shines? asked Billy.

'No.' said Mike.

John felt his face go red.

'I didn't think you did. Well, they used to call us Shines because they said we used to shine shoes - shoeshine boys, see.'

John didn't, but nodded anyway.

'Yeah well that's why you'd call us shines,' said Billy.

'I thought it might be because you er, they er, had shiny faces... ' said John.

Billy burst into laughter. Billy liked to laugh. John felt daft but he would rather feel that way than the way he had before. When he'd heard the kids talking about the Js and the Shines he never knew that's what it was.

'What about Js, what does that mean?' asked John, 'That sounds smart, that, the Js - like American, was that why the other gang called themselves that. Was it short for something... like, abbreviated?'

'Yeah,' said Mike. 'Abbreviated; we've done that. So was Js short for something? I know – Jets. Were they called the Jets, the other gang?' Mike looked chuffed. Billy smiled at him. Mike must have guessed right. 'Sod,' John thought, he knew he would have got it.

'Is that what it is then? It is, isn't it? asked Mike

'J.B.' said Billy

'What?'

'J.B. John Bull.'

'What's that mean?'

'Well the J is for John, so we'd call you John Bulls or Js.'

'Who's soddin' John Bull?' asked Mike.

'I'm not too sure. One of the older lads showed me a picture of John Bull who was a little fat fella with a Union Jack on his jumper or waistcoat. He had a bulldog with him as well.'

'I never seen no bulldog when I used to come up here,' said Mike. 'I seen a few Alsatians, but no bulldogs.'

'No it's not that; it's what I was saying this John Bull was like; it wasn't a photograph that I'd seen. I don't know really, I suppose it was like... a drawing, a cartoon.'

'Well I haven't seen him on the telly,' said Mike.

'No.' Billy was ready to laugh.

John felt like laughing as well but he didn't know why. John wasn't too sure what Billy was going on about.

'No, what I meant,' said Billy, 'it was like, do you know,' he paused, 'like Andy Capp – yeah, like a cartoon out the newspaper.'

'Well, what was he? asked John.

'I don't really know. I think he might have lived years and years ago, or maybe he never.

'Well, what about his bulldog?' said Mike.

'Ah hey, I don't know everything. I don't know why he had a friggin' bulldog. It was a load of shite, anyway,' said Billy. 'All that fighting; all them lads trying to make a name for themselves, getting chased by the police, going around showing off knives, carrying sticks with nails in them, trying to kill each other just because a school's getting built where they live. And I bet you some of them were going to go to the school as well. Bleedin' daft trying to murder each other, for what?'

John didn't say anything, although he'd believed the lads he'd watched were hard cases. But he wasn't sure now. What Billy said made it sound like it was all a bit daft.

John and Mike exchanged looks.

John thought Mike was thinking the same as him, but you never knew with Mike. The boys crossed the road. They walked on and ate some more sweets. John turned around. The sun hung over the Welsh Mountains.

'Do you like living down our way?' asked Mike.

'Yeah, it's alright,' said Billy. 'Like I said before, the house is good. Where we used to live was in a flat and you had to share a lavatory and bathroom with others in the house.'

'That's last that though, sharing,' said Mike.

'Not that bad; the people in the flats kept the toilet and bathroom clean.'

'Nar, still wouldn't like that.'

'Well, you didn't have to go out in the rain like the one in your back yard.'

'So, I won't be going out in a backyard when we move, when we... ' Mike stopped; he'd done it again. He knew what he'd said, then muttered, 'sharing's last.'

John knew Mike hadn't meant to mention moving out of the street and he probably felt bad.

'What happened to the house, Billy? Did it get knocked down?'

'No, still there; someone else living in our old flat now, a young fella and his wife with three little kids. We saw them. They were waiting to move in when we were moving out; they seemed alright. My dad had a word with the fella; he told him he'd left a few bits an' bats, a few old chairs, a little back kitchen table and some other stuff for him. My dad said he could keep the stuff or give it away if he didn't want it. The fella was made up he started shaking my dad's hand. You could see they didn't have much. All the stuff they had was leaning against the railings outside the house - a couple of mattresses and that - some of the stuff was tied up in bed sheets piled in a pram. Didn't seem much, unless someone had dropped it off and gone for some more, but I don't think so.'

'Where'd ya like living best?'

'Well, Grafton House is good because there's more bedrooms and we've got our own toilet and bathroom. And some of the kids are alright but some of them can be a bit shitty. You know - trying to be hard, wanting to fight you. I'm not fussed - I'll fight them - but sometimes they call our Christopher. When I lived up this way I had more mates, but I'm not that bothered. My mam used to say I could get on with anyone.'

John and Mike didn't say anything for a while. John wanted to say something but didn't know what to say. So he just said the first thing that came into his head.

'Don't you bother going to Church?'

'Nar, told you before - waste of time.'

John felt stupid asking him when he already knew.

'D'ya know what, John?' Billy carried on. 'There was this woman who lived in one of the flats and she used to go to Church every Sunday. And you know what? She was on the game.'

'On the what?'

Billy stopped and looked at him 'You know?' He nodded his head to one side.

John didn't know.

'You *know*,' Billy continued,' she went to Church but she was on the game,' he nodded again, and this time Billy winked.

John knew it was to do with doing something that was wrong, and against the Church. He should know this; he'd have to work out the answer before Mike.

'What is it?' asked Mike, 'on the game?'

'Oh, I think I know,' answered John. 'I know – yeah, I know, Billy - you mean robbing off the Church. Yeah, robbing when she went to Church, off the Sunday plate - *that game.*'

He felt alright now. Billy expected him to know and he did; he had worked it out before Mike.

Suddenly Billy burst into laughter.

John's mouth dropped open. 'Soddin' hell,' he thought, 'we don't half keep this fella amused. What now?'

'What ya laughing at?' asked Mike.

Billy kept on laughing. He didn't stop; it was obvious he couldn't help himself. Mike glanced at John.

'What's wrong with him?' asked Mike.

'I don't soddin' know.'

'You'll piss your pants if you carry on like that.'

This made Billy laugh even more. He bent over; people on the other side of the road pointed. John didn't know what to do. He wanted to tell Mike to carry on walking but they couldn't really. Billy just couldn't stop laughing. After a while his laughter slowed down, then it stopped.

John looked at him. The thought struck him –'This fella's mad; a soddin' loony tune, He could cause murder up here. I didn't know he was like this. I wonder if we can lose him when we get up there.'

'No, what I meant was,' Billy was trying hard not to laugh, 'What I meant was she was on the game. Y'know, she went with men... like a prostitute.'

'What?' John and Mike shouted at the same time.

'What? A prostitute and she lived in your house?' said Mike.

'Never lived in our house. She lived in the flat over us; bit of a difference, you know.'

'Yeah well, bleedin' hell, ah eh, I don't believe you. You're having us on again, aren't you?'

'No, why would I wanna have you on? I mean it's just that John was going on about Church and I remembered Mrs. Shaugnessy. She went to Church but she went with men as well, that's all.'

'I bet it wasn't a Catholic Church,' said John.

'It was - Saint Philip Neri. I used to see her in there sometimes when I was taken to Church.'

John didn't like that; he didn't like it, not one little bit. He wondered if Billy was joking. He could be, but he didn't sound like it. So he made something up.

'Yeah, but you know what? She might have went to a Catholic Church, Saint Philip thingy, but that doesn't mean she was a Catholic. Sometimes people who aren't Catholics pretend. Some of them even go to Holy Communion!'

'Well, why do they go if they're not Catholic?'

'I don't know Billy, how do I know?'

Billy smiled. 'Well if they wanna be Catholics and they're pretending to be Catholics... maybe that's the same as being one.'

John didn't appreciate Billy's logic at all. He knew he had to say something, but he didn't know what. Then it came to him.

'No! No! You can't be a Catholic just because you go to a Catholic Church. No, because you've got to be christened a Catholic - yeah, and make your first Holy Communion, then get Confirmation and go to a Catholic school and... '

'This is all soft, this,' said Mike. 'Listen, did you see her doing it, Billy - did you see her?'

John was glad of Mike's intervention, as his attack on Mrs. Shaugnessy needed more thought.

'What do you mean?' Billy asked Mike.

'Y'know,' said Mike.

'I know what?'

John knew what Mike meant. Mike nodded his head towards Billy. John looked around. On the other side of the road a young mother stopped; she held onto a pram as a small child held onto her other hand. The woman and the child looked across at them, turned away and carried on walking.

'Y'know, y'know,' said Mike, 'go on tell us, we won't tell no one, will we John? We won't tell. So go on, did you see her?'

The boys stopped to cross Windsor Street.

'Did you see her?'

'Yeah.'

'Yeah. Ah great, tell us.'

'Yeah, I seen her everyday and in the night.'

'Every day! Every night! Bleedin' hell - tell us, go on, go on.'

'I seen her going the shops, coming in the flat, going out, getting the bus, going... '

'I don't soddin' mean seeing her every bleedin' day like that. You know I meant doing it.'

'Doing what?'

'Y'know.'

'I don't, tell me.'

Mike leaned forward and whispered, 'Shaggin'.'

'Shaggin'!' Billy shouted it out at the top of his voice.

The woman with the pram stopped, then quickly turned around, pulled at the child's hand and hurried away.

'Bleedin' hell Billy, keep your voice down - you'll get us locked up,' said John.

'Is that what you was talking about, Mike?' asked Billy.

'Er, er - yeah Billy, but it doesn't matter now.'

'You've asked, so I'll tell you.'

John never asked; he didn't want to know. He glanced around to see if anyone was near by and told himself if Billy started all that shouting again, he was off. He'd go the rest of the way on his own.

'I never seen her, said Billy. 'Never even heard her, but that's what people said. But anyway, what's the big deal?'

'Well, she was a prostitute wasn't she?' Mike didn't realise he was whispering.

Billy bent his head towards Mike and whispered back, 'Was she?'

'Ah, you're just making it up.'

'I don't know if she was; that's just something the lads said. She was alright with me. She said hello and that never did me any harm. She gave me money if I went to the shops on a message. If anyone in the flats cut or hurt themselves, she'd patch them up with a little first aid kit she had; she knew what to do. She was good like that.'

John didn't know what to say. All he knew was what the gang in the street said they read in the Sunday papers. He didn't know what to say, but he had to say something because Billy had told them Mrs. Shaugnessy went to a Catholic Church.

Billy caught sight of the look on John's face.

'Look, sometimes she never had a job and lent money off my dad, but she always paid him back. She went out with a couple of different fellas and we seen them come out of her flat of a morning, so she went with men; that didn't make her a bad person.'

'She won't get to heaven if she's a prostitute.' As soon as he spoke John told himself to shut up. He tried to improve his argument, 'Doesn't matter if she goes to mass or goes to communion.' Even as John spoke he knew he sounded daft for going on about the Church.

'Well, I don't know about going to heaven, John, said Billy. 'What's it like? I've never been.'

Mike laughed. 'That's a good one that - never been,' he said.

This made him feel worse, especially with Mike laughing. 'Soddin' empty head Mike,' John thought. 'It's my own fault; I've got to learn to shut up.'

The boys crossed the road and talked about seeing The Beatles. None of them had a watch but they guessed it to be around four o'clock.

'Did you know The Beatles used to sing with a group from around here, The Chants?' said Billy.

'The Chants, from around here, a group like The Beatles?' asked John.

'No, they're coloured and never played instruments.'

'Well how can they be a group then?' said Mike

'They'd sing harmonies. They were good mates of The Beatles.'

'I don't believe ya,' said Mike.

Billy shrugged.

They turned into Berkley Street and Mike talked about the chances of getting his picture in the paper or on the television,

John only half-listened as Mike and Billy talked about which were their favourite Beatles song and their records being in the hit parade and seeing them on television, and how long the plane took from London. He considered Mrs. Shaugnessy. Would Billy tell them if he saw her? What did she look like? He should have asked Billy when he had the chance. Then again, probably better that he didn't. Billy might have carried on saying, 'Why, do you wanna go with her on a date, because she goes to Church?' Stuff like that, taking the Mickey. He told himself to learn to keep his mouth shut; put a zip on it.

They turned into Upper Stanhope Street, Mike and Billy still talking about The Beatles.

'Did you know,' said Billy, 'that The Beatles had the top five records in America?'

'Who told you that?' asked Mike.

'Our Sheila. It's great that, isn't it Mike? Top Five all at once.'

Mike was puzzled; so was John. He thought about it. 'Were they different records; was that it?' John was about to ask Billy was that how The Beatles had the top five records, then he noticed a crowd at the top end of Upper Stanhope Street.

'Look - something's happened.' It looked as though there had been a road accident. A policeman's helmet could be made out amongst the crowd, which had its back to the boys. John guessed they were looking at the crashed cars. He couldn't see an ambulance, though. As the boys drew nearer it became obvious the crowd was a lot larger than it had first seemed.

'Billy,' said John.

'Yeah, that's it,' said Billy.

Then, without a word, the boys picked up their pace, then they jogged, and finally they ran.

Chapter Nine
BEATLES

A child becomes an adult when he realizes that he has a right not only to be right but also wrong.

Thomas Szaz, *The Second Sin*

At Princes Road it was mad.

There were thousands of fans. They were everywhere. Most were in their teens, but there were also kids with their mothers and dads. Some of the kids sat on their parents' shoulders.

There were kids holding pictures of The Beatles cut out of magazines; some held the pictures high above their heads. Some waiting fans had plastic cowboy hats on, similar to those sold at seaside resorts with pictures of The Beatles pinned around them. Others had scarves with the names of the group knitted into them and some even wore Beatle wigs.

John thought that they'd got there too late, and that they weren't going to see The Beatles. He was sorry he'd come now. He could hear cars go by on Princes Road but he wasn't able to see them. He couldn't even see the road; all he could see were the backs of the fans.

None of the boys spoke as they walked around, half-dazed, trying to find a viewing point. But it was difficult to walk along the pavements, never mind getting to the front of the crowd. And it would have been no use trying to be hard-faced and pushing their way to the front: there were large numbers of older lads around and the boys knew they'd only end up being punched.

John couldn't help thinking it was their own fault, as they'd walked around trying to find a good place to see from. They shouldn't have taken their time, stopping and gabbing.

The only other time John had seen crowds like this was when he went to Anfield to watch Liverpool play. But then he had moved with the crowd, ready to pay his entrance money at the turnstile. He couldn't pay anyone here. He was convinced they'd never even catch a glimpse of The Beatles. There was nothing to see but waiting fans.

Then John remembered Billy's spec. 'Billy! Billy!' he said. 'Where's that spec?'

Billy didn't seem pleased to be reminded about his promise, but he told John and Mike to follow him. They went back the way they'd come, away from the crowds. Billy walked backwards, so John and Mike followed suit. They reached a point where they were able to see over the heads of the crowd and then Billy said, 'There y'are!'

John and Mike looked in the direction Billy pointed. On the other side of the road, a curved stone stairway swept up to the doorway of a church. It was a good spec alright - anyone standing there could see right above the heads of the waiting crowds - but the problem was it was already full of kids. They were everywhere: on the steps; standing on the wall; some of the little ones sat on the older ones' shoulders; others shouted to the crowd and waved their arms. A small boy held up a cutout cardboard guitar decorated with pictures of The Beatles.

The boys retraced their steps. They walked along Berkley Street towards Upper Parliament Street, but when they got to the junction where Upper Parliament Street met Princes Road it was the same: crowds of waiting fans were everywhere. Near the junction on the other side of Princes Road there was a large Victorian old peoples' nursing home. John stared at it. The upstairs had low-level sash windows that were all open wide, the nurses and the patients waved and smiled to those waiting in Princes Road. John's mouth fell open when he saw a resident, a woman, in her eighties sat in a wheelchair that had been placed close to an open window. She wore a wig, a Beatle wig. She looked mad. John nearly cried in frustration. 'The soddin' old ones were going to see them', he thought, 'and we weren't, it wasn't fair, bleedin' well wasn't.'

They dragged themselves through the crowds half in a daze.

'Let's go to the top of Upper Warwick Street,' said Billy.

The boys walked then turned left and along a street that ran parallel with Princes Road. They ate their sweets in silence; they didn't bother to swap. There was hardly anybody around, only a few old people who sat on the steps of the large terraced houses. Some of the old ones sunned themselves as they talked. The houses they sat outside were old and shabby; some of them had lines of bells on the doorframe; flats. John had been along this street before with lads from school, but he had never noticed the houses too much until now. It was like a Sunday morning - hardly anyone around - and now he could see how rundown and tatty looking they were. The houses had cellars surrounded with railings, but most of the railings were broken; some of the gaps between the railings were tied up with wire but most were left open. Some of the houses had windows which were broken and had been repaired with cardboard. The paint on the doors and the windows was old as well; on some houses the paint on the doors was made up of different colours, showing where repairs had been made. The chimneystack of one house leaned so far it looked as if it was ready to tumble down. Some of the houses looked ancient to John; they looked like they should have been bomdies ages ago.

The boys turned left and headed to the junction of Upper Warwick Street and Princes Road. It was the same. Crowds of waiting fans were everywhere. John had given up.

'What about getting to the other side of the road?' said Mike. 'It could be better. We could squeeze in and say we're just gonna cross the road.'

'What about the cars?' asked John.

'Why you worried did you forget to bless yourself coming out like your mam told ya?'

'Ah shut up Costello!'

'You'll have to watch out for "poey" vans.'

'What does that mean?' asked Billy.

'It's nothing,' said John. Sometimes you can tell lads too much.

'Tell him,' challenged Mike.

'A Post Office van knocked me down the other month.'

'What happened?' Asked Billy.

'I was playing with Bernie Owens in the schoolyard after school. Bernie was chasing me and I ran right out through the gates and there was a poey van coming down the street and it hit me.'

'What happened?'

'Nothing, it just hit me. I was alright, knocked me over, hurt my leg a bit.'

'What did your mam say?'

'Nothing.'

'Why?'

'I never told her if I did she'd bleedin' kill me.'

'Yeah, you're right.'

Mike butted in and spoke to Billy again about trying to get to the other side of the road but John wasn't listening. He though of how he ran out the school without looking. The next thing he knew he was in the air. He felt like he was flying. He fell down not faraway from where the van stopped. The driver jumped out of his van. Bernie had tripped and fallen as he avoided colliding with the van and lay sprawled in the middle of the cobble-stoned road. John half –sat-half-lay on the pavement and looked as the driver spoke in a panic to Bernie. The driver thought it was Bernie he'd hit. John sat up and watched as the van driver rubbed Bernie's leg. 'Hey it's me mister, you bleedin' hit me, rub my friggin' leg,' John said more to himself than to be heard. Bernie pointed towards John then the driver came over and asked how John was. He told him he was alright. The man lit a cigarette walked back to the van climbed in and drove off. John made Bernie promise not to tell anyone what happened.

'We've got to do something,' said Mike. 'It'll be last if we've come all this way and don't see them. What about going down towards Prinny Park? Maybe we can find a wall to stand on, or railings to climb up.'

'I think all the specs have gone now,' said John.

'Well *you* think of friggin' something, John,' said Mike, half-shouting.

But John had had enough of Mike. 'If you're gonna think of something,' he snapped. 'think of something proper.'

'What d'ya mean? Something proper? It's your friggin' fault anyway.'

'What is?'

'You made us get here late, ya friggin' soft get. Ya friggin' mammy's lad.'

Suddenly John wanted to kill Mike. 'At least I don't look like a friggin' canary with its head on back to front.'

John and Mike glared at each other.

'Fuckin' Holy Joe,' spat Mike.

John took a step towards Mike, but forced himself to stop. 'At least I can read a book without putting my finger under the words.'

Billy laughed.

'Fuckin' button your lip, Cleary, ya stupid bastard!' Mike shouted.

'I'm a stupid bastard?' said John. 'Here y'are what about this Billy. Last summer we went down the Dock Road me, Jackie Ryan and soft arse here, and there were these big letters on a wall of this mill, they had grain in there and all other stuff, it used to stink.' John talked faster with every word. 'The letters were big about six feet high, C.W.S. Me and Jackie Ryan didn't know what they stood for but he did, and he told us. I thought that doesn't sound right, so I asked my dad that night and he told me. Co-operative Wholesale Society, *C. W. S.* Do you know what he said it stood for? C. W. S. Cows' White Shit. An' me and Jackie believed him. He said the factory behind the wall, made stuff from it. He said their Steve told him that's what the smell was. If that's what your Steve said he must be as fuckin' soft as you!'

Then Mike did it.

John should have known what would happen. The frustration of both boys bubbled up and boiled over.

Mike dropped his head, ran and butted John in the stomach. Then he was on top of him, aiming punches at John's face. John was winded but he still managed to throw punches towards Mike's face; the boys' arms collided.

John grabbed the sleeve of Mike's jumper and tried to pull him off him, but there was too much give in the jumper: it just stretched and stretched and Mike never moved. John thought, Soddin' hell, he's like Elastic Man out of the *Fantastic Four*.

Then Mike caught John with a punch in the face. John tried to knee him off with his left leg and Mike almost toppled, but didn't. John tried to kick Mike with his right leg but it was pinned down. Mike caught him with another punch to his neck as John struggled, again, to knee Mike off him. John caught Mike with a punch and Mike went over on his side. John twisted from his back to his side and tried to get up, but Mike kept him down.

The boys pulled at each other as they lay side to side, kicking. John caught Mike with a kick to his ankle, pushed him, then he climbed on top of him and aimed a punch to his face, but Mike raised an arm and he hit that instead. John caught Mike with a hard punch to his shoulder. Then they heard the sound of a man's voice and John found himself lifted up and dragged away.

'Knock it off!' said the voice. 'Stop it, the pair of you. Stop it now!'

'Hey mister, you're hurting my neck!' said John, as he turned and saw that the man who was holding him was black.

The man grabbed the top of John's arm.

'What's going on?' he said. 'What are you fighting for?'

Neither Mike nor John answered.

The man turned to Billy. 'And what about you? Why didn't you stop them?'

'*Me*? Nothing to do with me. They're mates, aren't they? They're best mates. They were only messing about; playing.'

'*Playing*! They were trying to kill each other!'

Mike stood up. John stopped himself from looking in his direction in case Mike thought he was trying to make up. Instead he kept his eyes on the man. Even though it was a hot day, the man wore a shirt, a tie, a hat and a Mac buttoned up with the belt cinched tight. The man let go of John's arm and spoke to them all.

'Go on, get on your way home,' he said. 'And I'm going to watch you walk down the street. If you start again I'll call a policeman. Now, go on.'

The boys walked off. John looked straight ahead but he could see, from the corner of his eye, that Mike was folding the bottom of his jumper inside itself.

When they came to the end of the street Billy turned round and said, 'He's still there, that fella, watching us.'

Billy shouted back at the man. 'It's alright, mister. It's alright now. They were only messing.' Billy waved to him.

The boys walked on and John realised he felt better. Sometimes, when he'd had a fight, he felt better. Unless he got battered, then he felt last. But if he'd won, or it was a draw or, sometimes, even if he'd lost but had done alright, he felt better. What he didn't like about fights was waiting to fight. When he had to fight someone after school and the other lads were talking about it before it happened, or if there was a fight arranged at school on a Friday afternoon for the following Monday, that was the worst. But having a fight was nothing really; he'd been in lots of fights. It was just the waiting that was bad.

John recalled his first year at the juniors in the playground after school another boy from his class, Terry Foley, was trying to take a toy soldier off a lad from the infants. At the time John was scared of Terry who was bigger than him and always swearing. John told Terry to leave the lad alone but he wouldn't. Terry twisted the lad's arm and snatched the toy soldier off him; that's when the lad cried. The next thing John knew he had punched

139

Terry right in the mouth. He didn't even know he'd done it until he saw Terry fall on his backside. John looked at him splayed out on the ground, then at his fist. He couldn't believe it. He remembered being scared and angry at the same time. Terry dropped the soldier and the lad picked it up and ran off. John ran as well. He even ran past the lad, he ran like mad. He was scared as he ran but at the same time he also felt like laughing. That night he thought: 'Ah well I'll have to have Terry Foley a fight at playtime or four o'clock, that's it.' He accepted Terry would probably win but he wasn't too bothered. He was glad he'd done what he'd done. But when he went to school the next day Terry didn't say anything to him. John was a bit proud of himself although he never told anyone what happened. In his eyes he'd hit Terry, knocked him down but he also ran off as well, so it was nothing to brag about. At the time he was scared of Terry but not afterwards, not now. So fighting can be alright sometimes. John didn't hate Mike now the way he did before. Mike's his mate; he knew he was going to miss him when he went to the outskirts.

'I didn't mean that before,' said Mike, 'calling you a soft get.'

'Neither did I … saying you looked like a canary.'

They stopped walking and faced each other. This was the part John didn't like, making up. After they'd stopped wanting to punch each other's head's off they had to kiss the gob off each other. John thought it would be best if, after a fight, you didn't see each other for a day. Then you could forget about it. But sometimes that wasn't possible. Like now.

'I'll tell you what,' said Billy, 'I'm glad I came up here with you two. I feel safe. Any trouble and there'll be no problem with a pair of killers like youse.'

John wasn't sure if Billy was serious or just taking the mickey. He looked at Mike. Mike smiled. And then they both laughed.

'Still mates?' said Mike, and put out his hand.

'Yeah, best mates,' said John.

They shook hands and although John felt a bit of a phoney, but he knew that's what you had to do, especially if you were mates.

They doubled back towards the crowds, stood on a corner and looked around. Then someone shouted, 'Mo! Mo! Hi! Hi! Mo. Mojo!'

The boys turned and saw two black lads coming towards them, waving.

'Dennis! Raymond!' Billy shouted.

Billy didn't look at John or Mike as he walked over to the lads. John and Mike stayed where they were. Billy and the lads half-shouted at each other in a friendly way. One of the lads wrapped his arms around Billy and lifted him up; the other one gave Billy's shoulder a small punch. Billy did the same back.

John was about to speak to Mike but didn't in case Billy and the other lads thought he was talking about them. He thought of taking his sweets out but didn't. If the lads saw him eating a sweet they might think he had money, and from where John stood they looked a lot bigger than him. So John and Mike waited and said nothing until Billy walked back to them with the lads behind him.

'These are my mates from up here,' said Billy. The lads both looked older by a couple of years.

John and Mike said, 'Alright,' and the lads nodded. Then there was a silence between them until John asked, 'Do you live far?'

'Why?' asked the taller one.

'Just asking.'

'What's your mate got on?' The other lad said.

John looked at Mike. He'd forgotten about the jumper. *Bleedin' hell,'* 'Why don't you ask him?' John forced himself to reply.

'He looks like a banana,' said the taller lad.

The lad took a step and went to put his hand on Mike's head. Mike moved away.

'What're you doing?' asked Mike.

'I'm seeing if I can peel a banana.' He laughed and so did his mate.

'Good one,' said his mate.

'You think you're funny but your face beats ya,' said Mike.

The lad didn't like that. Billy's mates glanced at each other. John couldn't look away from the lads even though he wanted to. The thought of offering them a sweet crossed his mind but that would be the worst thing to do now.

'So have you heard, Raymond,' asked Billy, 'or what about you, Dennis - when are The Beatles coming?'

John had totally forgotten about Billy. His nerves had gone; he stopped looking at Raymond and Dennis and turned towards Billy who stood at the side of his old friends. Raymond, the taller of the lads, glared at John and Mike. John went to put his hands in his pockets but stopped; he didn't want to move.

'Someone with a tranny radio said they'd be getting here soon,' said Dennis. 'All the crowds have made them late.'

'I think we've got up here too late, haven't we John? said Billy.

'Yeah, I think so.'

'That your name, John?' asked Raymond. He looked at Dennis. 'John lar, JB lar, JB lar.'

'Yeah man,' Dennis said, 'John the JB.'

'Yeah, look at John the JB, lar,' said Raymond.

John's day had gone from bad to worse and now he didn't care.

'If I'm a JB, what does that make you?' But he knew as soon as he said it, he shouldn't have.

'Ya What? Ya little shit,' said Raymond.

John knew he was going to have to fight or run off. Uncle Jim had told him there's nothing wrong with being afraid. Breathe deep. that's what Uncle Jim said - that's what boxers do. He tried to take a deep breath but nothing happened; he couldn't. Uncle Jim told him even world champion boxers were afraid at times. Fear can be good, he had told John; it keeps you on your toes. The secret is not showing it. That's the hard bit about being scared - not showing it, that's what Uncle Jim had said. So here was the hard bit.

'Fuck off, Raymond,' said John.

Billy quickly stepped in between Raymond and John. Billy faced Raymond. 'Where are youse gonna see The Beatles from?' asked Billy. 'Have you got a good spec?' Raymond or Dennis never answered or acknowledged the question. Billy continued, 'Got any ciggies on ya, Raymond?'

Raymond glared at John from over Billy's shoulder, his eyes locked onto John's face, daring him to look back. It seemed like Raymond didn't hear Billy's question. There was a long pause before Raymond replied.

'Yeah,' he still glared at John as he spoke, 'but I'm saving them 'till after.'

John knew Raymond wanted to batter him; beat him up. But it was too late now; he'd said what he'd said and that was it.

'So, where are you going to be seeing them from?' asked Billy, again.

'We've got a smart place, really good. Never guess where,' said Dennis.

'Where?' asked Billy.

'My cousin Tony's going out with this girl and she lives in a flat on her own along Prinny Road. Her window looks right out. It'll be great.'

'Do you think we could come?' asked Billy.
John's head spun around towards Billy. His mind raced. 'What's he talking about. I'm not going anywhere with these bleedin' two, no chance, you must be off your soddin' head Billy.' Although he looked at Billy, John kept an eye on Raymond.

Billy and Dennis talked some more but Raymond didn't say anything, he kept looking at John. John wanted to go the toilet.

'Nar, ya can't come,' said Dennis. He spoke to Billy but looked at John and Mike. 'If you were on your own, might of... but nar. Got to get back now, or we might miss them. See ya, Mo.'

Raymond and Dennis left. Billy turned on John.

'What d'ya have to go an' say that for?'

'What?'

'Telling him to fuck off. You could have got us battered. They'd kill us, them. Raymond's the second cock of their year. I thought you were supposed to be clever?'

'But they started it,' said Mike.

'You're just as bad,' said Billy. 'It doesn't matter who started it; you're up here now, not down there. I know we're up Prinny Road but they wouldn't have done nothing. They were just showing off, trying to be hard. What if The Beatles' cars were going to the Town Hall along the Dock Road instead of Prinny Road and Raymond and his mates went to watch? They'd get done in down your way.'

'They wouldn't,' said John.

'Come off it, John. I live down there. They would, and you know it. It's bad enough that you get called all kinds when you're outside where you live. But you're coming up here where they live and calling them. That's daft that; stupid. For someone who's clever, you're not very smart.'

'Alright, tell them when you see them again, I didn't mean it,' said John.

'What? Like you're *sorry*?'

'Yeah, that's it.'

'John, if I see them again and tell them that you're sorry, they'll just tell me to fuck off. They'll think I'm soft. Just forget it.'

'They started it, though,' said Mike again.

'They didn't really, Mike, and that crack about your face beats ya didn't help.'

'That's a thing, Mike,' said John. 'You never said much after that, did ya?'

'What d'ya mean?'

144

'Well, you went quiet after that. There could have been a fight there. What would you have done?'

'I would have done something.'

'Like what?'

'Something.'

'What?'

'I would have run to your house to tell your mam where to send the ambulance.'

John wasn't too sure if Mike was serious or joking. Billy laughed; Mike did as well. John didn't in case his legs started shaking again.

'We're wasting our time here,' said Billy. 'Let's go back the way we came.'

John thought he'd done alright against Raymond, but now he wasn't too sure. He couldn't really argue with what Billy had said but these things happen and it didn't seem like he could do much about it. Then later on he might think, would he do that again? But that's the way things are. He didn't want to meet Dennis and Raymond. It wasn't his fault they'd seen them. But nevertheless, John guessed Billy was right. Maybe if he'd offered Raymond and Dennis a sweet straight away that might have been better or maybe not. One minute he thought he'd stood up for himself - he hadn't shown that he was scared - the next thing he was feeling like a divvy, and he still wanted to go the toilet.

'Maybe we'll get on the wall by the stairs,' said Mike.

'No chance,' said Billy. 'We won't get a good spec now. You heard them. The Beatles are going to be here any time now.'

John was angry. He wished The Beatles had stayed in bloody London. At that moment he hated them.

'There's James Hill there, John,' said Billy.' Look, I think he's with his mam.'

John looked over. Billy was right; it was James, James the Snitch.

'Who's that?' asked Mike.

'Some lad from our class. He got John the cane from the headmaster a couple of weeks ago.'

'What happened?'

'It was nothing,' said John

'Tell us,' persisted Mike

'Well I had some cards in the class and James Hill told Mr. Jackson and I got the stick; that's it.'

That's it; John had been given four of the cane because of what he'd said to James Hill. Mr. Jackson told the class at the start of the lesson that the boys weren't allowed to bring any Mars Attacks cards into school to swap or show off. Most of the boys in the school collected the cards. The cards showed a series of coloured pictures. One side showed different acts of the Martians invading Earth. On the reverse side of the card a brief story explained the scene. The cards were shocking and bloody, and not surprisingly the school didn't take too kindly to depictions of Martian spaceships firing at the soldiers, burning them up. Or Martians getting their bulbous brains shot at and blown apart, or family dogs being roasted alive by Martian ray guns, but John and the other lads who collected the cards thought they were great. Mr. Jackson had told the class that anyone with any cards should bring them out to his desk; he hadn't mentioned about returning them after school. Some boys had looked in their pockets and desks and brought the cards out.

John, who was sitting next to James Hill, had said more to himself than to James, 'What right do they have to take the cards from us?' James Hill had immediately put his hand up.

'Sir! Sir! John Cleary said what right have you got to take his cards?'

'Come out here, Cleary.'

'Yes, Sir.' John stood up and went to the front of the class.

'Did you say that?'

'Yes, Sir.'

'And have you got any cards?'

'Yes, Sir.'

'Well take them down to Mr. O'Boyle and tell him what you've just told James Hill.'

John went back to his desk, lifted up the lid and took the cards out. Everyone looked at him; they knew.

In Mr. O'Boyle's Office John repeated what he had said to James Hill; it was the same as the other times.

'Haven't I got better things to do than to deal with you, lad? Well! Haven't I?'

'Yes sir.'

'Cane and punishment book. You know where they are; bring them here.'

The punishment book and cane were always in the same place, on a window ledge by a statue of Our Lady. John put the cards next to the statue then it was 'four of the best.' Mr. O'Boyle would always say to the boys after he told them to put their hand out, 'This hurts me more than it will hurt you.'

John had wanted to say that day, 'Well here ya are, give me the cane and you hold your hand out - I'll save you some hurt, save you some pain. Go on, I'll do you a favour.'

Because it wasn't fair; he knew he shouldn't have been given the cane for that, not four. Sometimes John knew he deserved the cane, but not for that.

John trailed ten yards behind Mike and Billy as they looked for possible gaps in the crowd, but his heart wasn't in it and he looked around at the old and decrepit houses that surrounded them. When he mentioned to his mother, the route The Beatles were taking from the airport to the Town Hall, she told him lots of people with money used to live around Princes Road, 'Years ago a man wouldn't be seen without his cap on in Princes Road.' He glanced again at the houses. That *must have been* years ago because now the area was really rundown.

Then, he stumbled over a broken paving slab. As he picked himself up he noticed a torn, crumpled piece of newspaper lodged between half a house brick and a crushed tin can. And something was poking out from inside the newspaper. He reached for it and saw that it came from the racing section. Then he saw two crinkled £1 notes. His eyes widened as he unfolded the £1 notes and dropped the newspaper.

'Look,' he stopped in mid sentence. Raymond and Dennis appeared out of a shop on the other side of the road. They looked over towards the boys; Raymond held a bottle of lemonade. John froze.

'Hey Billy, here lar,' shouted Dennis.

Billy hesitated then slowly walked over. John slipped the pound notes into his pocket without taking his eyes off Raymond and Dennis.

Mike glanced over, then looked around and talked of trying to squeeze through the crowds.   John only half-listened. Billy talked to Raymond and Dennis and then cadged a cigarette off Raymond. Dennis lit it for him. Raymond and Dennis raised their voices but John couldn't make out what was being said. Raymond stopped talking and glanced over at John and Mike. Mike continued to search for any gaps in the crowd and talked about The Beatles. Raymond had put an arm around Billy's shoulder and pulled him into his chest as he spoke. John kicked Mike's foot, but never took his eyes off Raymond.

'What?' said Mike as he looked over, 'Oh oh.'

'Yeah!'

'What d'ya reckon?'

John didn't answer. He kept his eyes on Raymond.

'Do ya think Billy's still mad at us?' asked Mike.

Still John didn't answer he watched as Raymond spoke again to Billy, then let his arm fall from Billy's shoulder.

'Hey John,' Raymond shouted over. 'JB, come here, lar. I wanna talk to ya. Come on, I won't do nothin'.'

John told himself, 'Too right, you soddin' well won't because I'm not going, get lost.'

'Here y'are, man. Here y'are, lar; have a swig of my lemo,' shouted Raymond. He took the top off and held the bottle out.

John shook his head. Raymond spoke again to Billy. John didn't know whether to shout to Billy that Mike and him were leaving. That would have meant Billy having to walk home on his own and it didn't seem right, but he wanted to get away. Something was going to happen. He was about to speak to Mike, but when he turned to him it was obvious by the look on Mike's face he knew as well. John turned back. Mike followed his stare. Mike didn't like it. John didn't bleeding like it either.

Billy, shook his head to something Raymond asked. Dennis stepped in front of Billy and spoke to him. Dennis had his back turned to John and Mike. Billy nodded, Dennis stepped out of his way and Billy slowly made his way back. John and Mike didn't speak. John knew whatever it was, whatever Billy said, it didn't matter; him and Mike we're going to have to run, and run fast. He was tempted to look around to see which was the best way to run but he didn't dare; he had to keep his eye on Raymond.

Billy came towards them, head down and hands in his pockets. He reminded John of a gun fighter, someone out of Gunsmoke. 'Reach for the hole in your pocket' John thought, 'and pull your willy out the hole and fire when you want.' John told himself to, 'pay attention and stop thinking shite.'

Billy was a few yards away from the kerb, and still hadn't raised his head or said a word.

'Grab 'em Mo!' shouted Raymond.

John and Mike turned and ran. John didn't look around but he knew Billy was behind him. He heard him running. They ran away from Princes Road, Mike in front. They ran along Windsor Street. Toddlers playing on the pavements watched as the boys were chased. John and Mike crossed to the other side of the road. Mike ran into a block of tenement flats. John panicked; Mike didn't know his way around this neighbourhood. The door to the backyard might be locked. John knew he'd have to follow. The rear door to the yard had been torn off its frame. He caught sight of Mike as he left the back entrance of the block. In the yard Mike turned left, in towards Hill Street. John heard Billy's feet echo in the block as he ran outside. Mike could be seen briefly on the backyard wall before he dropped down. John followed. Mike had waited for him. They ran along an entry between the flats and Saint Martin's schoolyard. The entry came out into Upper Hill Street. Mike turned left and John followed as they ran away from Saint Martin's School back towards Princes Road. John was confused, then guessed Mike was trying to outsmart Raymond, who might know a short cut through the building site and cut them off. John began to get a stitch in his side.

Twenty yards away, a young mother came out of a house backwards, pulling a small pram. She held a baby in the crook of her arm. The woman bounced the pram down the steps of the house onto the pavement. The pram blocked Mike's run. Mike swerved but John had to leap over the pram. He knew Billy would have to slow down or try to jump the pram as well. John didn't look around. They turned into another street with derelict houses on both sides. The houses had been boarded up with corrugated tin sheets; some of the houses had the slates on the roof missing. The houses were wide - three-storey terraces - a dozen steps leading up to their front doors. At the end of the street there was an eight foot high wall blocking the whole street off. It was too late to turn back. Mike dashed across the road. He ran up the steps of the last house. The corrugated sheet nailed to the front door had been ripped back at the bottom. Mike pulled at the sheet and squeezed through the gap.

John knew Billy was close. He didn't have to look; he heard him breathing. He turned, and Billy ran alongside and glanced at him.

'Better hurry up, John, or they'll get ya. Raymond'll be giving' you a swig of his lemo up ya arse.' Billy gave a small laugh, and then ran past him.

John nearly gave a nervous laugh as Billy followed Mike into the house. John had slowed down, the pain in his side worse than ever. He reached the steps as Billy's feet disappeared behind the corrugated sheeting of the door. He ran up the steps, bent down and grabbed the edge of the sheet. As he pulled it back he turned around. Raymond ran ahead of Dennis; they were thirty yards away. Raymond slowed down and held up the bottle of lemonade, ready to throw it.

'Gonna fuckin' kill you!' shouted Raymond.

Raymond ran a few more steps, took aim and threw the bottle. John turned to crawl through the broken door panel. The bottle smashed inches from John's feet. Lemonade and glass flew up and onto his hair and jumper. He jammed his head and then his shoulders through the broken door panel.

The house was wrecked. He was halfway in but was unable to move any further. He pushed himself forward, but nothing. He was stuck. He turned around; his jumper was snagged on the corrugated sheet. Behind him Raymond and Dennis moved quickly onto the steps. John heard a noise from inside and turned as Billy dashed down the stairs. He jumped down the last four steps and dashed towards John. Billy grabbed the top of his shoulders and pulled. John felt a hand outside grab his ankle as he flew inside; he landed spread-eagled on the floor. Billy fell, then instantly scrambled up. John watched him from the floor as Billy dragged an old battered armchair nearby and pushed it across the door.

'Gonna fuckin' kill you, Mo!' It was Raymond.

Billy grabbed John by the arm and pulled him up 'Come on.'

'You're fuckin' dead, Billy Mo!' This time it was Dennis who shouted.

Raymond and Dennis reached in to push the armchair out their way. Billy raced up the stairs. John followed.

They stopped running when they reached to the top floor. Mike waited for them in a back bedroom. The ceiling was low and most of it had been pulled or fell down. Bits of broken ceiling plaster and laths lay all over the floor. The sun shone through a large hole in the roof where slates and lead had been removed. The gabled end wall and its uncovered pitched top could be seen in the loft as it rose into an apex. Scorched floorboards from a previous fire surrounded a six-foot hole, which extended from the middle of the floor to the fire grate. John and Billy stood there panting. John walked to the edge of the burnt floorboards and looked down to the room below.

'What are we gonna do?' asked John trying to catch his breath.

Billy searched the room. In a corner, a metal frame of a single bed lay on its side. Near to it a small chest of drawers had been smashed. John walked to the window. They were forty-foot up and even if they wanted to there was no drainpipe to climb down. The backyard door had been kicked in and the yard was half full of rubbish. Mike looked down the burnt hole through the floorboards. Billy had moved to a set of wardrobes that had been built into the recess of the chimneybreast.

'You're dead all of yas. Fuckin' dead!' Raymond's voice came from the ground floor.

The boys froze.

A door was kicked open downstairs. John went over to Mike and looked down the hole to the floor below, half expecting to see Raymond looking up.

'What are we gonna do?' whispered Mike as he stared down to the room below.

Raymond and Dennis stamped their feet as they climbed the stairs. One of them banged what sounded like a stick, on the bannister.

'Gonna get yas! Gonna kill you JB!' shouted Raymond.

'An' you Banana Man!' this time it was Dennis, 'Gonna do you in Billy Mo! Good style.'

The banging on the bannister became louder and nearer. Raymond and Dennis were on the first floor.

Billy opened the doors to the wardrobes and looked in. He closed them.

'Shall we try to run down the stairs?' whispered Mike.

Billy kept moving and looking around the room. The sound of a door being kicked downstairs made him stop. A windowpane below smashed. Billy looked up at the roof then moved to the bed frame. He lifted the frame up and propped it up against the wall. Billy pointed upwards as he looked at John and Mike.

'We'll climb up,' said Billy.

'What?' said John.

'Not long now Billy Mo!' shouted Raymond. They were on the floor below. A door being kicked open made Mike jump.

'We'll climb onto the ceiling joists,' said Billy, 'then walk across them to the wall. Hide up there.'

John looked up to where the fire had charred the ceiling joists. The joists still looked strong enough but they ran across the burnt out hole in the floorboards.

'Come on it's easy,' said Billy.

'What if they're in the room below, look up and see us?' said John.
The sound of a stick being smashed on the floor echoed up the stairs. Billy and Mike never answered John or looked at him; instead they moved towards the bed frame. Billy steadied the frame as Mike climbed up. Mike pulled himself up onto the joists first kneeling and then standing he put both arms out to steady himself then walked across.

'Come on John,' said Billy.

'No you go it's alright Billy,' said John.

Billy reached over grabbed hold of John's arm and dragged him towards the bed frame. Again Billy steadied the frame as John climbed towards the ceiling joists. John gripped a joist. The metal frame slipped. Billy grabbed hold of the frame before it could clatter to the floor. John looked up. Mike was already on the other side of the room. John climbed onto the joists. Mike held onto the top of the wall and pulled himself up.

'So you're up there are ya Billy?' shouted Raymond.

John bent down from the joists and stretched out an arm for Billy. Billy tried to find a toe grip between the bedsprings and the frame. His foot slipped.

'Not long now Mo.' Dennis shouted. His voice came from the bottom of the stairs.

Billy found a foothold on the bed frame and pushed himself up, John grabbed his hand and pulled. Billy scrambled up. John straightened up turned towards Mike and held his arms out for balance. Mike stretched out on the inclined wall, hugging the sides. He caught John's eye and waved a hand for him to follow. John took a few steps.

'We're comin' for yas!' it was Dennis.
A stick banged on the wall as Raymond and Dennis climbed the stairs.

John stopped. Billy was balanced close behind him. 'It's OK,' Billy whispered. They moved together. As they crossed the hole in the floorboards John stopped. He couldn't move. Billy put one hand on John's shoulder while his other hand lifted John's chin up. 'Come on John let's go,' said Billy.

The banging of the stick told the boys Raymond and Dennis were in the next room. Mike held out his hand, John grabbed it and was guided towards the wall. Mike moved further down the inclined wall to give him room to mount it. John scrambled up throwing, first one knee and then the other onto the brickwork. Mortar broke away he looked down as it pinged down to the floor below and then through the hole in the floorboards to the next floor. He turned his head and looked out down into the street. Below was a waste patch of land. The twisted wheels of an old rusty bike poked out from beneath a pile of bricks. He turned back and lay flat, his face pressed against the brickwork, his feet near to Mike's face. Billy pulled himself up and moved above John. He lay down and stretched out flat legs towards him. The three boys lay head to toe. The sound of a stick hitting the bedroom door forced John to screw his eyes shut.

John heard footsteps in the room and opened his eyes. He could see the legs of Raymond, the section of the ceiling that was still up partly hid the boys. Raymond and Dennis moved towards the side of the room where the boys were. Raymond held a stair spindle. He crept around the room. Dennis went towards the hole in the floorboards and bent down. He had his back to the boys he straightened up, turned and lifted his head up to the open ceiling. John held his breath.

'Dennis,' whispered Raymond.

Dennis spun towards Raymond who stood by the wardrobes; Raymond put a finger to his lips. As Dennis walked over, Raymond took the spindle off him and nodded for Dennis to grab the wardrobe doors.

'Now!' shouted Raymond.

John let out his breath.

Dennis pulled both doors open.

'Shit!' said Raymond and kicked the doors.

Dennis went towards the window and looked out.

'Raymond.' Dennis waved him over and pointed.

'Yeah I can see,' said Raymond, 'the back door. Come on let's go or we'll miss The Beatles.'

Raymond flung the spindle away, as they left the room and ran down the stairs. John looked mesmerized as the spindle hit the fireplace below him and bounce onto the burnt floorboards then through the hole down to the room below and out of sight. Billy adjusted his grip on the sides of the wall. John's knuckles were white with holding on. The boys listened as Raymond and Dennis kicked at the corrugated sheet and made their way out the front door.

From behind him, John heard pieces of mortar fall to the floor below. He held onto the wall tighter as he turned around. Mike looked at him with a wide-eyed stare. More mortar bounced down to the floors below. Inch by inch Mike slid away from him. Mortar and small pieces of brickwork came away from where Mike held on. Mike's hands seemed to be stroking the sides of the wall. His mouth was open as if to ask a question, he slid further away. John went to speak but nothing came out. He opened his mouth wider and took a deep breath preparing to shout but couldn't. He tasted dust and soot. He shut his eyes tight, bit his lip and found his voice, 'Billieee!'

Billy turned, looked towards John and Mike then twisted himself around and jumped up in a crouch.

'John!' shouted Mike.

Billy stretched over John and crawled towards Mike.   Mike's feet were near the end of the wall he tried to get a foothold and pushed at the brickwork a loose brick came away and tumbled into the yard below. Mike tried again to push himself back up with the toes of his shoes, more mortar and brickwork came away and he continued his slide.

Billy's head came level with John's shoes.

'Grab me John,' said Billy.

John held onto Billy's legs. He pressed his knees onto the sides of the wall for a better grip.   Mike held on with one hand and reached out with his other.   Billy pushed out his hand to Mike's, their fingertips touched then Mike slid further away.   Mike's feet dangled over the edge of the wall.   Billy stretched out some more. John released his grip on the wall and inched himself and Billy down towards Mike; he pressed his knees against the sides of the wall as hard as he could.

Mike thrust out his arm again. He jerked his body towards Billy's hand. He missed.   Billy stretched down further.

'Again!' shouted Billy.

Mike slid further down the wall. John held tighter onto Billy's legs. Billy heaved his body down the inclined wall as Mike stretched out again.   Billy caught his hand.   Mike stopped sliding.

'The other hand,' said Billy.

Mike looked at the hand, which held the side of the wall.   Slowly he moved it from the wall and pushed it towards Billy.   Billy grabbed Mike's wrist.

John caught sight of the twisted bike wheels below, he squeezed his eyes closed and pressed the sides of his feet against the wall with all his strength.

                    *   *   *

The boys sat on the steps of the derelict house, John on the top step, Mike and Billy on the next step down. Their clothes and hands were covered with dust and dirt.

Billy told them that Raymond and Dennis told him to grab and hold onto John and Mike, or they'd beat him up.

'I thought they were your friends,' said John.

'So are youse,' replied Billy.

Mike threw a stone at the lamp post that faced the steps. He missed. He put his elbows on his legs and his chin in his hands.

A mangy-looking dog sloped towards them.

John checked his jumper to see if it had a hole in it. It did.

The dog stopped near the bottom of the steps. It tilted its head and looked up at the boys then it cocked its leg against the lamp post and pissed.

'That's it then,' said John. 'We've missed The Beatles. Let's get off.' He stood up.

'No, we haven't,' said Billy. 'Look around.'

Except for the mangy dog, the street was deserted.

'There's nothing here. No one's around,' said Mike.

Billy stood up. 'That's what I mean,' he said. 'If The Beatles had already been, we'd see some of the crowd getting off home, we haven't missed them yet.'

John went down the steps two at a time. He turned back to Billy. 'It's friggin' hopeless,' he said, but he was smiling.

'It's not,' said Billy, smiling back at John. 'I know it's not.' He banged the dust from his clothes.

Mike and John did the same.

'Come on,' said Billy, 'follow me.'

He began to run.

Mike followed.

And so did John.

Chapter Ten
CATHERINE STREET

Ringo: I want to see my solicitor.
Desk Sergeant: What's his name?
Ringo: Well if you're gonna get technical.

A Hard Day's Night, Screenplay

The boys ran back the way they had come. Mike asked Billy where he was taking them but Billy wouldn't say. They came to where they'd first seen crowds; it looked like the crowds had grown even larger. The boys ran towards Princes Road and stopped twenty yards short of it. The kids that surrounded the stone stairway seemed to have grown in number as well. The boy with the cardboard guitar was still there. The neck of the guitar had snapped; it flopped down, although the boy tried to keep it straight.

'Let's get off, come on,' said John.

'No, wait there,' said Billy. 'Look, it's no good here, is it? We're never gonna see them; we're not gonna see nothing. What Dennis said before got me thinking. Dennis said they're gonna watch from a window, yeah? Well what do you reckon *we* watch from a window? I can't promise nothing, but we can try.'

'That sounds great; where's that?' Mike was excited.

John was as well, but he didn't want to build his hopes up.

'Come on, let's go' said Mike. 'Where is it?'

'Mrs. Shaugnessy's,' said Billy. 'The Beatles cars will go right past her window.'

Dear God! At first John thought he had misheard Billy.

'What?' said Mike, 'That woman that goes with men?'

'Yeah.'

'Oh no, I'm not going. Nar, not me,' said John. 'I'm not going. Flippin' 'eck, I don't fancy that, Billy. I think I'll go home first. Nar, I'm not going.'

'What's wrong, John, you're not scared are you?' asked Billy. 'You just had a fight with Mike, nearly had a fight with one of the hardest lads around here, ya could have broke your neck on them joists and you won't go in some woman's flat with your mates to look out of a window. You're bleedin' mad, you. What are you scared of?'

'I'm not scared, it's just... '

'Well if you're not scared, let's go then,' said Mike. He rubbed his hands.

John was fed up; all these people - kids, daft sods with wigs on making a show of themselves. Anyway, he reasoned, he wanted to go to the toilet. He wondered if it was because of what had happened with Raymond; no, he needed to go.

'I'll get off. You go, I'll see ya later,' said John.

'Come on,' said Mike. 'If we hurry up, wc'll scc them. Come on.'

'Nar, you go.'

'Come on - you're up here now, aren't ya?' said Billy. 'Be alright, honest - not messing, be alright.'

'Nar.'

John walked away, confused and frustrated. He knew he'd get a smack when he got home, but that didn't bother him. He wanted to go with Mike and Billy but if his mother found out, that'd be all he'd need. Mike would say he wouldn't tell anyone that they'd gone into Mrs. Shaugnessy's house - he would swear on his grandma's grave, swear on his granddad's grave - but he would, he'd tell. Mike couldn't hold his own water, never mind keep a secret.

'John! John! Here,' shouted Billy.

159

John stopped. Mike and Billy came towards him.

'What about this, John?' said Billy. 'You don't wanna be walking back home on your own, do you? So look, come with me and Mike and if she's not in... well we'll walk home with you; we'll all go home together. Because we're not going to see anything if we don't get into Mrs. Shaugnessy's so it's not worth staying, is it? What do you reckon?'

'Come on John,' said Mike.

'Yeah, alright,' said John.

They opened their bags of sweets, then swapped and ate the last of them. Billy told them where Mrs. Shaugnessy lived. It was a continuation of Princes Road, but the road narrowed and its name changed to Catherine Street when it crossed Upper Parliament Street. The boys made their way to the end of Berkley Street then towards the traffic lights at the junction. They walked in the road because there were so many fans on the pavements. The crowds were the same in Catherine Street; any space that was on the steps that went up into the houses on Catherine Street was taken up with waiting fans.

He noticed that the houses were old but not rundown or shabby looking, like those behind Princes Road. The houses were three storeys with small iron verandas on the middle floor; they had large sash windows and wide doors. Outside each doorway stood a pair of stone pillars that supported a pediment. Most of the windows on both sides of Catherine Street were open and had people leaning out. Some of the windows on the upper floors had bed sheets with messages written on them: 'We Love You, Please Please Me'. Many of the sheets had The Beatles names along with hearts and kisses. Another sheet had 'Come on By My Love'. It reminded John of the record he had bought. He wondered who he could give it to; he didn't want it now. He might be able to swap it.

The boys finally pushed their way to the house. A group of eighteen to twenty-year old fans stood on the steps that led up to the front door. They looked at the boys as they stopped at the bottom of the steps. The boys were given a look, which told them not to try to push up onto the steps.   John felt crap; even worse than before. He was going to miss The Beatles and if Mrs. Shaugnessy were in he'd have to walk home on his own.

Billy tried to move onto the step. He had to squeeze through those already there who didn't like it and wouldn't move. Billy pointed to the set of bells on the doorframe and some of those who stood on the steps turned towards where Billy pointed. They reluctantly parted to let him move to the door. Billy pushed a button.   When he did, he knocked into one of the lads. The lad pushed his face into Billy's and said something that John couldn't hear. Another lad looked at his watch. John considered asking him the time but didn't in case he thought he was only making conversation in order to move up on the steps. He waited to see if the door would open, then that was him; he was off. He wanted the door to open for Mike and Billy but at the same time he didn't want it to open for himself. He looked around and again thought of the best way home. He turned back around as the door opened. Mike moved behind him.

John turned towards him.

'I'm getting off now Mike, see you later.'

'No, wait there. Billy's got some money for you - he said Mrs. Shaugnessy owes him some money, for going on messages for her or something, he's gonna get it off her and give it to you for buying us the sweets.'

'What are you going on about, Mike?'

'Mike!' it was Billy.

Mike grabbed him and pushed him up towards the door, Billy rushed down the steps, grabbed John's arm and pulled. John stood on someone's toes as he was dragged and pushed up the steps. Those waiting on the steps shouted and swore as they were jostled. Before John went through the door he heard one of them say.

'Wash your pockets.'

John thought, 'Bleeding cheek, wash your pockets; we're not dirty.'

Mike shut the door. The hallway was thirty feet deep. Two front doors to the flats faced the stairs. Underneath these sat a pram.   A couple of unopened envelopes lay on top of a small cupboard near to the front door.

'What do you think you're doing?' said John, 'You two are soft - you could have ripped my shirt. My mam would have killed me.'

'It's alright - we didn't, did we?' asked Billy.

'No!'

'I've asked Mrs. Shaugnessy could we come in and watch from the window and she said yeah. I told her you were a bit shy. She's upstairs now; she's leaving the door open. Come on.'

'We planned it,' said Mike. He had a wide smile and looked chuffed. 'Me and Billy planned it when you were walking away. We only did it 'cause you know, like Billy said, you're a bit shy and that.'

'I'm not - I'm not. I just didn't wanna come, that's all.'

'Well we're here now,' said Billy. 'Come on, let's go up, if you're not shy.'

'No,' said John.

'Why?'

'That's why.'

'Are you and your friends coming up, Billy?' Mrs. Shaugnessy, shouted down from the landing above.

'Are you coming then?' asked Billy.

John wanted to go and he didn't. But he felt ashamed after what he had thought about Mrs. Shaugnessy and what he'd said. John wasn't too sure if he wanted to see The Beatles from Mrs. Shaugnessy's. He did, but... he wanted to but... he just felt... he didn't know. Billy grabbed his arm and pulled him towards the stairs. John let him. Mike grabbed his other arm.

The stairs were wide; the bannister a deep, stained, polished oak supported by a diamond-patterned ornamental wrought iron, painted black. Billy talked about seeing The Beatles while Mike talked about being on television or in the paper because of his jumper. John took a quick look at him and hoped Mrs. Shaugnessy had a sense of humour. As they climbed the stairs he looked around. Dark green linoleum covered the hallway floor and the centre of the stairway. It was old. In places the floorboards showed through where the linoleum had worn out. And the walls had marks and scrapes in places that revealed the plaster beneath. It smelt a little musty but not too bad; it was clean. He didn't think it would be this good. The doors on the landing didn't have doorknockers or letterboxes; buttons for the doorbells were fitted on the surrounding frames. The doors were painted light blue. Small plastic door numbers were set high in the centre.

On the second landing, Mike turned around. 'Come on,' he said and stopped.

Billy carried on walking.

'Come on, I'll wait for you,' said Mike.

John saw an open door. 'He'll wait for me,' John thought, 'because he's scared, he doesn't want to go straight in. He wouldn't wait for me if it was a sweet shop and they were giving away free sweets.'

'Yeah, I'm coming, now,' said John.

Billy went straight into Mrs. Shaugnessy's. He didn't knock first or give a shout. John thought that was hard-faced, but then again Billy said Mrs. Shaugnessy was easy going. A cat padded past the boys and down the stairs.

'See that,' Mike pointed and spoke with authority. 'Mice, that - that's for mice.

John wanted to say something but never.

'You alright? Not scared are you, John?' Mike asked.

'No, I'm alright.'

John had a good look at Mike for the first time since they'd left the street; a jumper on back to front. Mrs. Shaugnessy won't know if he's coming or going. The folded bottom of the jumper had now slipped right down. It looked like if it were pulled, the jumper would come down below Mike's knees. The holes where the elbows used to be seemed to have grown even larger. A back to front 'v' neck sewn up; she'll call the police and get him locked up; he looked like he's just escaped.

'Shall we go in?'

'Go on then.'

They went in and stood in a narrow hallway. There were three doors. One door was partly open to the left and Billy's voice could be heard from there. A further door faced them while the third stood partly open to the right at the end of the hallway; it was the kitchen. Mike went towards the sound of Billy's voice and John followed.

Billy and Mrs. Shaugnessy were talking together near a large sash window that overlooked Catherine Street. Mrs. Shaugnessy had her back to John and Mike. Her hair was bobbed and red, and she wore a green dress. Billy gave Mrs. Shaugnessy news of his family. John looked at the high ceiling with an ornate plaster frieze; a brass crystal chandelier hung from the centre of a ceiling rose. John wanted to have a good nose around the room but he didn't want to be caught. Getting caught didn't stop Mike. His eyes were everywhere; it looked like his head were on a swivel. John looked at him. *Bleeding shameless*, Mrs. Shaugnessy definitely won't know if he's coming or going if she turns around now. John stared straight ahead and looked at the fireplace. It was old fashioned but not like Annie Hood's. Mrs. Shaugnessy's fireplace was a dark oak. Carved acorns and leaves wound their way up the sides and below the mantle piece.

'And these are my mates,' said Billy.

John turned as Mrs. Shaugnessy looked towards him and Mike. To him she looked ordinary. Just like a woman you would see in the street. She wasn't as old as his mother but she was older than Mary. He guessed she must have been about twenty-five - thirty?

She had a nice face, not pretty but not plain. She looked like a woman you'd see in a shop or somewhere. Ordinary. Familiar.

'This is Mike and this is John,' said Billy. 'You'll like John; he's going to be an altar boy.'

John felt his face burn up. Soddin' hell Billy!

'Nice to meet you.' she smiled, 'Would you like a cup of tea or would you like some orange juice?'

'Yeah,' said Mike, 'orange juice.'

To John, it seemed as if Mrs. Shaugnessy looked at him like she knew what he'd been saying about her and the Church. He knew, she knew. *Bleedin' hell; Billy's told her what I was saying about her, about her not being a Catholic but going to Church and what she's doing is wrong, oh soddin' hell.*

'And what altar are you going to serve on, John?' asked Mrs. Shaugnessy

'What?'

'Billy said you're going to be an altar boy.'

That's it, she bleedin' well knows. She knows I know she knows, all what I said about her. Billy's told her. And Mrs. Shaugnessy looked at him. And he definitely knew she knew.

'Er, er 'he couldn't speak; his mouth felt like blotting paper. He told himself to swallow. Try swallowing; he did. 'Er, Saint Pat's. Saint Patrick's.'

'That's nice. I'll go and get your orange juice.'

He was sorry he'd come now. Mrs. Shaugnessy left the room. John felt better. When he looked around, Mike and Billy weren't there. They'd gone over to the window. Billy pushed the sash window up and leaned out, Mike went to the window as well. John followed them.

'Billy, did you tell Mrs. Shaugnessy what I said about her?'

Billy half turned, 'Said what about her? What are you talking about?'

Mike nudged Billy and pointed into the street. Billy stuck his head back out the window and shouted below for news of The Beatles. As he did John gazed around the room. There was a three-piece suite and a sideboard cabinet with ornaments inside. A large round polished table with carved legs sat in the corner of the room surrounded by four matching chairs. Pink flowered patterned linoleum covered the floor. A rug was placed in front of the fire. The walls were painted a light yellow. The sun came out from behind a cloud. Sunshine shone into the room and onto the crystals of the chandelier that created patterns on the walls and ceiling. He knew that the room must face west, like his bedroom. He looked towards the fireplace again. A carriage clock sat on the mantelpiece next to a framed photograph. He went over to look at it. The picture was of Mrs. Shaugnessy with a baby boy. Mrs. Shaugnessy was younger, her hair shoulder length. They were on a beach. The sea could be seen in the background. Mrs. Shaugnessy held the child up high above her. The photograph reminded John of what footballers did when they won the cup. The child was laughing and Mrs. Shaugnessy smiled. The frame was silver with heart shapes in each corner. A child-sized crucifix and chain hung on one corner of the frame. He noticed an open manila envelope near to the frame. On it sat a bill. John stood on tiptoe to peer at the bill; it was a final reminder from the Electricity Board. He wondered if Billy was telling the truth about Mrs. Shaugnessy or only joking. He wasn't too sure. He wasn't really bothered any more. He wanted to look at the photograph longer; he wanted to pick it up, but didn't in case he was caught nosing by Mrs. Shaugnessy.

He went over to Mike and Billy and pushed his way in between them.

'There's thousands here, isn't there?' said Mike. 'Look, see that fella there - he's got an umbrella with all The Beatles' names painted on the top. Look, they're waving to us from that window - they've got a good spec as well, like us. It's great, this!'

Mike was right. It was great. Hardly any pavement space could be seen. Any walls that gave a vantage point had fans sitting or standing on them. One lad, John's age grinned as he sat on top of a pillar-box that faced Mrs. Shaugnessy's. The lad held a large piece of cardboard: 'We Luv The Beatles' had been written on it. The boy saw him, waved and held up the sign. He waved back.

Above the roofs opposite he saw the top of the Anglican Cathedral. The spires that circled the top of the cathedral reminded him of a crown of thorns. The cathedral was three hundred and thirty one feet high. A builder's crane could be seen at the far wing; the completion date for the cathedral was still nearly twenty years away. Three hundred and thirty one feet was big, even for a cathedral.

Uncle Jim had told him of the different workers that had helped build the cathedral: master stone masons, lead light makers, marble floor layers and master carpenters; some of the men had worked on the site for thirty or forty years. He told him that what people think is the front entrance to the cathedral is really the back. The side that faced Mrs. Shaugnessy's was intended to be the front. On that side was an old cemetery, situated in a disused quarry. It ran the length of the cathedral a hundred foot below the level of Hope Street. The intention was to build a bridge over the cemetery giving access to the cathedral. On that side of the cathedral were the houses of merchants, ship owners and cotton traders. The bridge was for those who had contributed to the building of the cathedral. But those people had begun to leave Liverpool and the money intended for the bridge went with them. So they used the entrance on the opposite side. When his uncle had told him about "the rich ones", he had raised his voice.

'Great, isn't it lad? They made that much money out of trade from the city; millions of pounds they made, they had that much they could afford to build their own cathedral and wanted a bridge - a bridge and an entrance - just for themselves! All the money they made from hardship and poverty through the work on the port; then they have the cheek to build their cathedral with its back to the river!'

John's mother had come in from the parlour to see what was going on. Uncle Jim had stopped talking. John's mother had returned to the parlour and Uncle Jim had spoken again.

'I don't want to bring you down, son, with tales like that. Listen to what your mother and dad tell you and then work it out for yourself. You'll know what's right and what's not. You won't go too far wrong. Just remember, there's good and bad everywhere. And think for yourself - don't have others thinking for you.'

John didn't like it too much when Uncle Jim talked to him like his mother. It was best when his uncle just told stories.

Mike pushed himself further out of the window and shouted to those below. John leaned out as well, but as he bent forward he felt a pain in his stomach; he'd have to go the toilet, and soon.

'She's alright, that Mrs. Shaugnessy, isn't she John?' said Mike. 'She's got a smart house.'

'Yeah, she's alright Mike.'

'She told Billy that The Beatles are about half an hour late. There are loads of girls at Speke Airport, but they should be here soon.'

'Here's your orange juice,' said Mrs Shaugnessy.
The boys turned. Mrs. Shaugnessy had three glasses of orange juice on a tray.

'Would you like a biscuit?' asked Mrs. Shaugnessy. She sat the tray on a small table near the window.

'Yeah, great,' said Mike. Mrs. Shaugnessy noticed their hands as they took their glasses. Mike finished his glass of orange juice in one swallow.

'Would you like to wash your hands?' asked Mrs. Shaugnessy.

'Nar,' said Mike.

John nodded as Billy shook his head.

'There's a sink in the kitchen, I'll show you.'

Mrs. Shaugnessy walked towards the small hallway. John stood at the sink as Mrs. Shaugnessy passed him a bar of soap. She looked at his dirt-covered hands. He noticed her look.

'We met some of Billy's mates. We were playing with them.'

168

'So, you attend mass at Saint Patrick's? That's Monsignor Curry's Parish, isn't it?'

'Yeah,' said John, surprised she knew,

Mrs. Shaugnessy opened a cupboard door and pulled a packet of biscuits out. She moved towards a stack of plates as John rinsed his hands. Mrs. Shaugnessy stood next to him.

'I'll get you some more orange juice to drink,' she said.

John moved away as Mrs. Shaugnessy filled three more glasses up with water. He looked around the kitchen. On a shelf were half a dozen ceramic jars and a first aid kit. Below, a small cork message board was fixed on the wall above a table and chairs. He looked at the slips of paper pinned to the board; a receipt from a pawnshop caught his eye. He moved half a step closer.

'Oh, I'm sorry,' said Mrs. Shaugnessy. 'Were you waiting for a towel? Here.'

He turned and looked down at his wet hands. Mrs. Shaugnessy spoke as she turned to get a towel.

'So, you're going to be an altar boy? Your mother must be very proud of you.'

John felt himself blush. He took the towel that she held out and quickly dried his hands.

'I'll get back to the others,' said John as he returned the towel.

Mike and Billy still leaned out the window. John pushed himself between Mike and Billy. As he did, Mrs. Shaugnessy returned with a plate full of biscuits and orange juice. The boys took a biscuit and fresh glass of orange juice.

'You'll have to give The Beatles a good cheer after coming all this way', said Mrs. Shaugnessy. 'Try to let them know you're there; give them a wave, they might wave back.' She looked over the boys' heads and out the window. 'Haven't you brought any scarves or pictures to wave? Lots of people have.'

John knew she wasn't being funny; she was only asking, just being alright.

169

'No,' said Billy, 'we haven't got nothing like that - no scarves or hats - but Mike's brought his jumper.'

Billy burst out laughing. So did John, then his biscuit went down the wrong way and he nearly choked and started coughing. Eventually, he stopped coughing and Billy stopped laughing.

'Yes, I can see that,' said Mrs. Shaugnessy. 'It's a fine jumper, Mike.'

Mike told her how his jumper was going to get him in the newspapers and on the television. As Mike spoke, Billy went back to the window and leant out. John needed to use the toilet; the orange juice and biscuit had made his stomach-ache worse. But he was too embarrassed to ask Mrs. Shaugnessy if he could, and where it was. Billy shouted to someone outside, then turned around.

'They're at the other end of Princes Road, by the Park. The Beatles are gonna be here soon.' Billy gave the thumbs up sign. 'This lad just shouted up.'

This made John want to go more.

'Billy I'll have to go the lav.'

'Well you'll have to hurry up.' Billy never turned around when he spoke.

'Yeah, but where is it?'

'It's on the next floor down; it's facing you at the bottom of the stairs, in the corner,' said Mrs. Shaugnessy. 'There are two steps down before you go in. You won't miss it.'

'Better hurry,' Mike shouted as John left the room and made his way into the hallway.

He *definitely* needed to go *now*; thinking about it had made it worse. At the front door he had to resist the urge to run, knowing full well that this would result in him cacking himself. He had to walk. On the stairs he went down sideways. I'm like a soddin' crab; this is bleedin' great, this.

On the next landing he saw the door set in the corner. It was closed. Carefully, he went down the two steps and turned the handle. The door wouldn't open. He tried again and pushed it, turned the handle and shoved the door with his shoulder; nothing. It must be stuck. He shoved it again.

'Won't be long, have some patience,' a voice said from inside the toilet. The voice sound like a small child's.

Bleedin' hell, there's someone in there. Oh soddin', shittin' hell, I need to go now.

'I'm nearly bleedin' cackin' myself,' John spoke through gritted teeth to the closed door.

'Have some patience; patience is a virtue,' the voice said.

He stared in confusion at the door. 'That's what my mam would say.' John thought, 'Friggin' hell, my mam's in Mrs. Shaugnessy's lav.' John nearly laughed. Don't, he told himself; 'you'll shit yourself. Don't.'

'Won't be long,' the voice said.

He pushed his legs together. Billy shouted down from Mrs. Shaugnessy's landing. 'Come on, John! The Beatles are nearly here. Ya can hear all the people shoutin'. Come on, they're comin'!'

'I can't get in!'

'Why?'

'Cause there's someone in there.'

'Oh well, come up here - you can use a milk bottle.'

'I wanna poo as well.'

'Ooo, you wanna pooooo.'

Bastard taking the soddin'... John said to himself, then half cried, 'Oh bleedin' hell, I don't half wanna go.'

'Well hurry up, anyway,' shouted Billy.

The toilet flushed. Come on, come on, come on. The door opened.

'Patience is a virtue, you know,' the voice said.

A very old and very small woman appeared from the toilet. She was smaller than John by a good three inches. He looked at her. *It's a wonder she never fell down the soddin' toilet, she must have had to put lead in her shoes to stop herself falling in.*

171

The woman took her time, slow. It seemed to John that she moved an inch at a time. He watched her shuffle up the steps. *It's the lead in her shoes, that's what's slowing her up, and here's me cackin' myself.* He had to move back up the steps to let her past. He kept his legs pressed together. He wanted to push past her as she climbed the two steps, but he might have knocked her over. If he did that, he'd have to bend down to help her up and in the process he'd probably shit himself, so he waited.

'There, that wasn't long, was it?' she said.

Not for friggin' you it wasn't, missus, let me in.

He rushed past her. Inside he pushed the door closed with his foot, then the zip. But he'd forgotten the pin keeping his zip up.

'Oh soddin' hell, my pin,' he half cried, 'the bleedin' stupid pin in my soddin' dungarees, get it out quick, quick.'

He found some cut-up newspaper on a shelf. Then he heard it, a loud roar. He pulled up his dungarees, opened the door and told himself to hurry up. He reached down to his zip, ready to run. Both hands were on his zip as he pulled it up and tried to push the pin in at the same time. Then he fell; he couldn't break his fall. He landed on his face. *The bloody steps*; John had forgotten about them. The noise was heard again, only louder. He jumped to his feet and ran up the stairs like a madman. Sod the pin.

He burst through the door. Mike, Billy and Mrs. Shaugnessy were standing near the window. When they turned around, John knew then; he *knew*. *I'm too soddin' bleedin' late.* He didn't know what to say. He stared open-mouthed at Mike and Billy. 'The bleedin' gobs on them;' he said to himself, 'you'd think they'd seen a miracle. You'd think they were with that girl who seen Our Lady at Lourdes; they're grinning the grin of the soft, daft bleedin' gets. I want to soddin' punch them.' Even Mrs. Shaugnessy had a smile. He felt soddin' last, totally confused telling himself, 'first I wasn't bothered, then I was, now this. It's bleedin' well not fair, it soddin' well isn't.'

'Ya should have seen them,' said Mike, 'just like on the telly; just like they are in the papers. Fab! That's it, they were

172

Fab! And ya know what, y'know what?' Mike was ecstatic and John bleedin' hated him.

'He pointed up at me,' continued Mike. 'He'd seen me - you could see his rings all over his fingers, just like on the telly. He saw me. He pointed at me.'

John glared at him. 'Yeah, probably thought what the fucking hell is he wearing, the soft-looking bastard. I know it's swearing, but I don't care Shit! Fuck! Bastard!' he nearly blurted out.

John felt bad because he had sworn. Mrs. Shaugnessy looked at John and smiled. No one spoke. The clock could be heard ticking. Mrs. Shaugnessy took a step towards the window and looked out. 'A lot of the crowd will be going into the town centre, to see them at the Town Hall. Are you going?'

'Nar,' said Mike. 'We've seen them now. They were *great*.'

'Well we'll get off now, Mrs. Shaugnessy,' said Billy. 'Thanks for that.'

Mike grabbed the last of the biscuits off the plate. John glared at him, *hard-faced bastard*. If it's free, it's for me. John bet Mike had that tattooed on his arse.

'Ta ra, Mrs. Shaugnessy,' said Billy. He turned to John. 'Your fly hole's open, John, and you've got a mark on your head. What happened, did you fall down the toilet?'

It wasn't even funny but Mike and Billy laughed, especially Mike. He glanced down; the pin was open and stuck in his dungarees. He was surprised it had never dropped out running up the stairs. He put the pin into his zip and fastened it up. He mumbled something about falling over outside the toilet, then rubbed his forehead. Mrs. Shaugnessy didn't say anything. John was the last one to the door. He looked at the mantelpiece, at the picture. Mike and Billy stepped into the hallway and talked about The Beatles.

'You might change your mind on the way home and maybe go to the Town Hall after all,' said Mrs. Shaugnessy. 'You could try to get their autographs. Have you got a pencil?'

Billy and Mike were talking in the hallway; they never heard Mrs. Shaugnessy. John shook his head.

'Well, let's see if we can find one; come on.' Mrs. Shaugnessy went to the bookcase. John followed and watched as she searched in between the books and amongst the ornaments. John glanced at the framed photograph of Mrs. Shaugnessy and the boy which faced him on the mantelpiece.

'Shall we go, then?' Billy shouted in.

And John thought 'no, I don't want to go. It sounds daft because I didn't want to come, but now I didn't want to go. I'd be walking home with them and all I'd hear was what The Beatles looked like in the cars, who'd seen who, who looked the best, who waved to who and all that, all the way home; they'll drive me 'round the bloody twist. That would be bad enough, but not only that I want to stay. Stay here and talk, talk to Mrs. Shaugnessy. Ask her, how long have you lived here? Do you like living around here? Or that photograph of you and the lad, is that your lad? It's at the seaside, isn't it? Where were you, Southport or New Brighton, or was it Blackpool? Who took the picture? Talk about anything. I wouldn't talk about Church, nothing like that. Not many people would let three kids in their house, two of them you don't know, and then give them orange juice and biscuits. All I want to do is sod the others off and sit on the couch and talk to her.'

John really wanted to stay, and he knew it wasn't going to happen. Mrs. Shaugnessy still searched for a pencil. John dug both hands into his pockets as he waited. He felt the pound notes he'd found half an hour before, partially pulled them out and glanced at the money. He looked again at the photograph and noticed the unpaid electric bill. John paused then slowly took the notes fully out while still half-looking at Mrs. Shaugnessy. He reached up towards the mantelpiece and placed the notes behind the picture frame.

'I've only got this,' Mrs. Shaugnessy turned and held up an eyebrow pencil.

174

He paused for a second, then took the pencil and put it in his back pocket. She walked him to the front door.

'Thanks for the orange juice and thanks for the biscuits.'

He didn't think he would be able to say it but he did, and felt a bit better and also strange. Strange in the sense that, in a way he really didn't know what he felt; he didn't know if he was sad or down or glad that he came or what... he just felt different, that's the only way he could explain it.

Chapter Eleven
HOME

Children have never been very good at listening
to their elders, but they have never failed to imitate
them. They must, they have no other role models.

James Baldwin, *Nobody Knows My Name*

Outside there was hardly anybody around. The pavements
that five minutes before were crammed with people, were now
empty, the only people around were a couple of policemen and a
Saint John's Ambulance man talking to each other on the opposite
side of the road. The litter from the crowd was the only sign of The
Beatles passing. Billy led the way he crossed over to the other side
of the street and down a road that ran towards the Cathedral. They
passed the post-box, where the boy who waved to John sat. The
cardboard sign that the boy had held reading 'We Luv The Beatles'
lay on the pavement scuffed and marked with footprints.

'See down this road,' said Mike as he pointed to the road
the boys were about to turn into, 'the last Rolls Royce left the
others and shot down here. Didn't it Billy?'

'It was a Bentley not a Rolls Royce,' said Billy.

Mike and Billy argued about what type of car it was then they
carried on where they left off from before about which one of them
saw the most. Next, it was how big the cars were, how many
policemen there were on motorbikes and which Beatle was in
which car, then they sang a Beatle song. John walked a few yards
behind. The street was wide. The houses double-fronted and larger
than those in Catherine Street. All the doors had polished brass
letterboxes and knockers, no bells. He noticed a road sign 'Myrtle

Street Children's' Hospital Turn Left.' He remembered the nurse in the hospital that would sing to the children. He would have liked to tell Mike and Billy about the nurse but they would have said he 'was soft in the head', 'cracked'. Maybe he was, sometimes he wondered. Mike and Billy continued to talk about what they'd seen. John wasn't bothered now; it's gone, sod it. He glanced around at the houses and thought what it must have been like to live here when the houses were first built. He guessed this was where the merchants lived, that Uncle Jim mentioned, those with live-in servants, butlers, maids and horses and carriages. At the end of the street, he caught sight of Hope Street and the railings that ran around the grounds of the Cathedral. He remembered, coming down this same street, a week before Christmas. It was dark then so he didn't notice too much where he was, especially after he had started running.

Each Christmas a party was arranged for the children whose fathers belonged to the Territorial Army. The party took place at the barracks in Aigburth Road. John had attended the parties ever since he could remember, mostly with Mary. But Mary hadn't been the last few years and his dad had just taken just him.

After the party John stayed behind. He waited upstairs in the barracks social club; the sign on the door said 'Officers Mess'. His dad served behind the bar and he had to wait for him to finish. That was the first time he knew that his dad served drinks in the barracks, even though he was the Regimental Sergeant Major. Most of those in the club wore dress uniforms with medals and were well spoken. His dad had a uniform on as well, but he didn't look the same behind the bar, he had his jacket off and a white waistcoat on. John recalled that when the officers ordered drinks they called his dad Cleary.

'Two pints and a double whiskey, Cleary.'

'A whiskey and soda, R. S. M. Cleary.'

He didn't like that. It was different when his mother or Uncle Jim called him that. He felt like saying something but never, instead he sat at a table on his own with a packet of crisps and a bottle of lemonade. He wandered around the room. A large painting of the Queen hung on a wall, next to it was a photograph of the Royal Family. John sat back down. There was nothing to do except watch his dad serve drinks and listen to the officers as they talked loudly about politics and where they were going on manoeuvres next summer.

John noticed one of the officers walk off after playing a slot machine. There were two slot machines in a corner. He had seen them before but they were always being played. Now no one used them, so he went over. One machine took shillings and the other sixpences. He wanted to play the machine. He'd never been in the club before and wasn't too sure if someone might tell him off. But he wasn't bothered. He had a couple of sixpences so he played the machine. *Sod them*.

The first attempt on the machine he won four sixpences, so he dropped another sixpence in the slot. Then another and won the jackpot, a pound's worth of sixpences. He almost shouted out in excitement. Men nearby turned at the sound of the sixpences as they clattered into the steel cup of the machine. Back at the table he put some of the sixpences in his coat that hung on the back of the chair

An hour passed and his dad came over to where he sat, it was now well past eight o'clock, John grabbed his coat ready to go. He told his dad about winning the money, he showed him some of his sixpences but his dad didn't seem that bothered. John thought he'd caused trouble for him with using the slot machine and he was going to tell him off before they went home but it wasn't that. Another barman was due to relieve his dad from behind the bar but hadn't arrived, so he'd have to stay. John would have to catch the bus home on his own.

From the bus stop where he stood he could see the windows of the Officers Mess. The sound of the officers' noisy conversation and laughter drifted down to where John waited.

He knew he had to catch the number Twenty Bus, which would stop, outside Saint Patrick's Church but instead, by mistake, he caught the number Twenty Five. He didn't know how he got mixed up. He knew he'd caught the wrong bus when it turned right instead of left at the end of Aigburth Road. He wasn't too sure which way the bus was going to go after that. He didn't want to ask the bus conductor where the bus was going because he would have felt daft, so he waited to see where it went. It went along Princes Road and then onto Catherine Street. When John saw the top of the Cathedral he rang the bell on the bus. As the bus pulled away he looked around, he wasn't sure where he was and even though all the gaslights were on along the street he was scared. It was cold. He could see his breath in the night air as he walked. When he reached the end of the street he turned left onto Hope Street. He picked up his pace. As he did he looked down into the cemetery that was laid out in the grounds of the Cathedral.

Even though it was dark, he could still make out the headstones and crosses on the graves. The wind whistled through the trees that were dotted around the cemetery. He walked faster. The cemetery had been there a hundred years before they began building the cathedral; some of the lads at school told him they'd seen ghosts there. He didn't really believe them ... but began to run anyway. But when he ran all the sixpences and other coins started jingling in his pockets. John thought, 'friggin' hell this is great, I sound like a moneybox falling down the stairs.' He ran faster but the jingling got louder, he told himself he couldn't stop and walk because someone might have heard the money and want to rob him. So he slowed down and quickly put all the money in his two side trouser pockets, then shoved his hands in, held on to the coins tightly and ran. The coins never jingled when he ran, so he ran faster. He ran, as fast as he could and the faster he ran the more John thought of the barracks.

*   *   *

He crossed over a road. Mike and Billy were twenty yards in front. They still talked loudly about The Beatles. Mike waved his arms about, Billy laughed. Then they both sang. But it wasn't them. He stopped. There was singing but it wasn't Billy and Mike. He looked down the road he'd crossed. Nearby was a wide entry that ran behind the houses. The singing came from the entry. He turned and walked towards the sound of the voices that sang in harmony. He looked along the backyards to the sound of the singing when a large black car slowly entered the top of the entry and drove towards him. The car was a Rolls Royce, it parked half way down the entry near to the sound of the singing, the driver beeped the horn, parked and switched the engine off. A man's voice came from behind the backyard wall, 'Here's your car.'

The second voice stopped singing. The driver stepped out of the car. He wore a chauffeur's uniform. John went towards the car. The chauffeur took a cigarette out and glared at John then waved him away. John stood there. The voices in the backyard spoke and then there was laughter. The chauffeur lit his cigarette took a step towards John and waved him off again as a latch was lifted on the backyard door. The chauffeur raised his fist at John. The backyard door opened and two men stepped out, their backs to John. One was a young black man dressed in grey slacks and a blue shirt. The other white, who wore a black suit, shirt and tie. Both were in their early twenties. The men looked at the chauffeur who lowered his fist, dropped his cigarette and stubbed it out. The young black man turned to face John and smiled, he looked at the man in the suit and nodded towards John. The man turned. John stopped breathing. He'd stopped breathing but it didn't matter. It was *him*. The man smiled, John tried to smile back but found his lips wouldn't work.

'Hiya what's your name?' asked the young black man. John didn't look at him, he couldn't turn his head but he knew he'd been spoken too. 'Would you like his autograph?' the young black man asked.

John thought he nodded but wasn't sure. He began to breathe again. The two men searched their pockets. The young black man pointed at the pocket of the chauffeur's jacket. The chauffeur pulled out a packet of cigarettes and threw them over. The young black man opened and emptied the packet. He winked at the chauffeur then tore at the packet and turned it inside out.

'Pen?' The young black man asked.

The three men shook their heads. John moved a step towards them and took out Mrs. Shaugnessy's eyebrow pencil.

John Lennon looked at it, 'Bit young for girls aren't you?'

John blushed and put his head down.

'Who shall I sign it to?' asked John Lennon.

'John,' said John.

John Lennon smiled, 'From one John to another eh?' He passed John his autograph and pencil. John Lennon shook hands with the young black man as they said their goodbyes. The chauffeur opened the car door, John Lennon climbed in. The chauffeur got behind the wheel and started the engine. John's eyes locked on to it until the car turned out of the entry and disappeared. He turned around. The young black man stood in the doorway of the backyard. He smiled, winked then closed the door. John looked at the closed door, then at the pencil and autograph that he held.

'John! John!' It was Billy at the other end of the entry, 'Come on! What are you standing there for?'

He looked once more at the pencil and autograph then put them in his pocket.

He didn't say anything to Mike and Billy because it didn't seem real and talking might break the spell. It was like a secret that once told would cease to be real. He couldn't think then when he could, he still didn't say anything. He didn't know why he just didn't. It might have been to do with the fact that he couldn't find the right words to say what he saw or how he felt. And with Mike and Billy not being there, it didn't seem right anyway.

They crossed Hope Street. Mike and Billy finally stopped going on about seeing The Beatles. The three of them talked about football and television, *Sugerfoot*, *The Terrible Ten*, *Deputy Dawg*. They argued in a friendly way about which was the best cartoon

The Flintstones or *Bugs Bunny*, and about their favourite toys and favourite sweets. They talked about anything.

The boys arrived at Park Place outside the Church and waited to cross the road.

'Do you know what you were saying about the priests getting buried, John' said Mike, 'remember when we used to dig a grave for dead pigeons? Remember we used to put a cross where we used to bury them, remember?

'What's all that?' asked Billy.

'Me and John used to go down the Dock Road and collect dead pigeons. You'd see them on the railway lines by the docks. The pigeons used to be after the corn and stuff that fell off the railway wagons that go along the Dock Road and they'd get run over by the trains, they mustn't have heard them coming. We used to wrap them in newspaper, take them back to our street, dig a hole on the Billy ock, and bury them. We'd get lolly-ice sticks and make a cross with string or that. John would say a little prayer, just messing an' that, it was alright, just something to do in the holidays, wasn't it John?'

'Yeah just something to do in the holidays,' replied John.

He was about to say that they were only kids then but he didn't. He wasn't too bothered if it sounded soft, they did it and that was that, only kids playing. He wasn't worried if Billy thought they were daft gets for collecting dead pigeons and burying them, that's what you do when you're little, everyone does daft things. Mams and dads do daft things just like kids do. Maybe when they do them they don't seem daft, only when they think back on what they've done, when things are different, later on when they became older; when things change, then they look back and think...

'Better get off,' said Billy, it must be getting on.'
The boys crossed the road.

They went down Hill Street and past May Brennan's. John wished he had some money left for sweets, not that he was hungry. He wanted to buy some as a reward for themselves especially Billy. When he passed the door John looked in to see if May or Joe were serving, he would give them a wave and they'd wave back but he never caught sight of them.

The boys didn't talk much. It was like there was nothing to say, they couldn't talk again about seeing The Beatles and him not seeing them because now that didn't seem right. But in a way Mike and Billy had to talk about it because that's what they went up there for. He knew it wasn't Mike and Billy's fault he never saw The Beatles, it wasn't their fault at all. He knew he couldn't mention his autograph because that would have in some way cheated Mike and Billy out of what they had seen. They were quiet then John thought of something.

'Billy, you know when you were trying to ring the bell at Mrs. Shaugnessy's what did that fella say to you?'

'What?'

'The fella on the steps he bent his face down to ya, what did he say?'

'I can't remember, I don't know.'

'I'll tell you what Billy, you've got a bad memory you, it was only before. Did the fella have a cob on with ya over something?'

'Oh shut up John.'

John looked at Billy. He'd upset him. He tried to think what he'd said... nothing he couldn't think of anything. Then he thought of something else.

'Billy.'

'*What?*'

John definitely knew he'd upset him now. 'Er, you know when we went into Mrs. Shaugnessy's.'

'You mean when we dragged you in,' said Mike.

'Yeah well, same thing, know when we went in, what did that fella mean on the steps' ''wash your pockets?'' 'Did he think we were dirty? Is that what he was saying to you when you rang the bell, is that it?'

'Is what it?' said Billy

'What I just said about, ''Wash your pockets.'''

'Bleedin' hell John. D'ya know what you're supposed to be clever but you're not half-daft. What he said was "Watch your pockets."'

'They thought we were gonna rob off them, try and pinch something and run,' said Mike.

'There y'are Mike knows,' said Billy, 'He's not soft.'

'Well why would they think that?' asked John.

'Because they were students, they think they're smart an' because they think we're scruffs.'

'How'd you know they're students?' asked Mike.

'I know don't I. I used to live up there.'

'Do they live around Berkley Street, around there?'

'No, that's where Raymond lives; the students wouldn't live there. The other side of Upper Parliament Street, that's where they'd stay. There's loads of them up there in the flats it's handy for the University. You can tell them by the way they dress, scarves or carrying books and by the way they talk. Definitely by the way they talk.

'Don't you like them?' asked John

'Nar... I mean some are alright but others can be a bit snotty.'

'How?' asked Mike.

'Well it wasn't what they said, it was... more the way they looked at you. They thought you were nothing. Not all of them, like I said, some weren't bad but sometimes you'd be in the shop and they'd be there and they'd look at you, look you up and down, sometimes just stare at you, didn't care if you seen them looking, maybe they thought they were invisible. You could tell they didn't rate you. Sometimes me, Raymond and the others would play football in the car park of the University. And sometimes we'd get chased by the people who worked there or sometimes by the students. Once we were playing and this student came out to get into his car, he started calling us, so we stopped playing. I had hold of the ball; we were waiting for him to go so we could start playing again. Then when he was backin' his car he stopped and wound his window down. He put his head out and shouted.'

"Keep that ball away from my car you dirty little beggar!"' 'That's what he shouted. I kept the ball away alright but I picked up a stone and threw it at his car, I didn't half hit it. Then we all legged it. They're not all bad but some of them are horrible; shites some of them.'

John and Mike looked at each other they didn't know what to say. John was sorry he asked him about it now.

They stopped again at the corner of Mill Street and Hill Street outside the same pub they'd talked about Biddy Hill over two hours before. Men would hang around on the corner after the pub shut in the afternoon or stand around waiting for it to open, or when they had no money. There was no one on the corner now, it was Friday and everyone had money. The boys gazed down Hill Street between the silos across the river and the Wirral. None of the boys spoke. John stared down at the roof of Billy's block and then at the Southern Hospital. There were no lorries or vans around; everyone had finished work. It was late, there was hardly anyone around. Mams and dads would be getting ready to go out while the kids watched television, *The Beverly Hillbillies*, Friday night. He glanced towards the sun. He was able to look at it without blinking. It seemed more orange than yellow with a pink haze around it. He knew it was late because the sun was past the old silo. He wondered what Mike and Billy would say if he said that it looks great, the way the sun was and the sky without any clouds and the way the silos made shadows across the houses and rooftops. They'd probably laugh, probably say he was cracked, daft; ah sod it, if they do they do.

'It looks good doesn't it,' John pointed towards the sun, 'making the shadows all over the place?'

Mike and Billy turned to the sun then looked at each other.

'Yeah you're right John,' said Mike, 'when you think about it, it is good.'

'I'll tell you what John,' said Billy, 'you're not often wrong but you're right this time. You know what that is?' He nodded towards the sun. 'That's beautiful. *Fabtastic.*' He gave a short laugh then turned away. Two men came out of the pub, stood by the boys and spoke to each other.

'Let's get off,' said Billy. They crossed the road and carried on down Hill Street. They talked about football and the television. Billy said *Bonanza* was on at seven o'clock; they'd be home for that.

And then they were back near Billy's flat.

Mike put his hand out. Billy shook it, and then he shook hands with John.

Mike and John watched as Billy walked off.

Mike talked about what it would be like to live up by where Billy used to live, the large houses and being near to the town centre but John only half listened. When they came to their street Kevin Dunleavy kicked a football against the gable end of his house.

'Where've you been?' he asked.

'Went up to Prinny Road,' said Mike.

'Did you see them? What was it like?'

'Yeah we seen them, didn't we John? It was great, loads of people there, thousands, millions. Did you know The Beatles had the top ten number one records at the same time in America? Did you? Did you know that?'

'No. Who told you that?'

'Our Steve.'

'What's with the jumper?'

'For the telly, we're gonna be on the telly, me, John and Billy Mogan. The cameras were there! You missed it. It was great! Great! Got to go now Kevin see ya later.'

John knocked at his front door, he knew he'd be kept in and smacked for sneaking out but when Mike asked, if he was coming out after tea. John said he was, just so as not to disappoint him. Mike said he'd see him later on as John's mother opened the door.

His mother told him off for coming in late and climbing out the window. He waited to be smacked but she hugged him and he knew he was in the wrong. She was worried about him. It was on the radio and the television that hundreds were hurt watching The Beatles landing at the airport. She told him, that even when The Beatles were at the Town Hall hundreds of fans were injured. She'd seen the Saint John Ambulance men on the television treating the fans that were crushed and injured; there were hundreds of thousands of fans there. She told him she prayed for him. She didn't shout and she didn't hit him, so she must have been upset. John supposed all mother's are like that it's just the way they are. His dad didn't say much. He put his newspaper down and told him he should have been home earlier as he had upset his mother. John couldn't look at either of them. He stared at the toe of his shoes and picked at the sleeve of his jumper.

All the wallpapering had been finished. None of the tears could be seen and the rolls all matched up. His dad and Uncle Jim had done a decent job. It looked fine. Peter had gone out with Uncle Jim and Mary was around at her friend's. They asked him what happened and why he was late. He told them they met some of Billy's old mates. And that they went to one of Billy's old neighbours, Mrs. Shaugnessy, that she was nice and that she let them in her house to see The Beatles drive past from her window and she gave them orange juice and biscuits. So he wasn't lying really. His mother asked him what the mark was on his forehead, she said it looked like a bruise and was immediately concerned until she rubbed it and found it was only a smudge of dirt. She told him to wash his hands and face then she'd do his tea, fish.

After his tea he read a comic then remembered about Mike leaving the street. 'Mike Costello's moving you know mam? Going to the outskirts.'

'Is he, when did he tell you that?'

'Today.'

'His mam's said nothing to me. When's he moving?'

'I don't know, he didn't say.'

'Whereabouts he moving to, does he know?'

'Halewood, some place called Maggots Lane.'

'Where?'

'Er, Maggots Lane... that's what he said anyway.'

John's mother looked at his dad.

'Maggots Lane, that's a funny name,' said his dad, 'I've heard of someplace that sounds like that. You say it's up in Halewood?'

'That's what he said.'

'I know now, there's a fella who I worked with, he's moving up that way, *Mackets Lane*, that's what it'll be, I think Mike's got it wrong.'

They looked at him but John didn't feel daft, he wasn't bothered, it's just one of those things, no one's perfect. He wondered if he'd be getting chased out of Mike's house after they leave, the way he was today in Jackie Ryan's.

The pin had come out of his dungarees; he'd never noticed his zip was half way down, his mother told him to go upstairs and change them, then she'd put the television on, *Bonanza*.

In his bedroom John took his dungarees off. Out of a back pocket, fell the pin he told his mother he couldn't find. He changed into a pair of trousers. He took the pencil and autograph out of his dungarees and went to the pictures of The Beatles. He tucked the pencil and autograph behind a picture of John Lennon, paused then took the pencil out, looked at it for a moment and went to the wardrobe. He opened the drawer and took out a maraca, the one that held Uncle Jim's union badge, pulled the handle off and placed the pencil inside, pushed the handle back and returned the maraca.

He went over to the window. The sun had disappeared behind the silos. He thought about when they came out of Mrs. Shaugnessy's and the sign for the Children's Hospital. When he was in hospital he needed to have injections and takes doses of medicine that didn't taste nice but it wasn't all bad. He'd rather have been playing out in the streets with his mates, but there were some good things as well. He wanted to tell Mike and Billy about the time he was in the hospital. He was sorry he never now. He would have told them about a nurse there, who was kind. He couldn't remember her name but at night, when no one was around she sang to the children. It was summer and when the children went to bed it was still light outside, the children would stay awake whispering to each other. The ward was out the way at the end of a corridor, so the nurse let the children climb out of bed. She would sit in a chair while the children formed a half circle around her on the floor and when they were all sat down she would sing to them. It would be quiet. The children couldn't hear anything in the corridors or even the traffic outside so she sang quietly. He could only remember one song. It was always the last song she sang, the nurse said it was by Frank Sinatra and called 'High Hopes'. She told the children she would sing the song to her baby as a lullaby. John remembered the song was about an ant and a rubber tree plant and the ant tries to pick it up but he can't, but he tries, that's the main thing; he tries. The nurse taught them the words to the chorus and let them sing it with her, but they had to sing quietly, and all the children sang: 'He had high hopes he had high hopes, high in the sky apple pie hopes.' All the children looked at each other and smiled and even though they didn't really know one another, they smiled like mad. They were smiling, even when they were singing. It was great. She told the children to get back into bed after they'd finished. The nurse had shoulder length red hair. She looked a bit like Mrs. Shaugnessy. And when all the children were back in bed, John would pull the sheets up to his chin and think, wouldn't it be great to feel like this all the time.

> 'Where d'you live?'
> 'Down the grid.'
> 'What number?'
> 'Cucumber.'
> 'What's your name?'
> 'Mary Jane.'

The things you say, when you're a kid.